Blue
Murder

Forthcoming

Classic Hard-Boiled

42 Days for Murder by Roger Torrey

Modern Hard-Boiled

The Blind Pig by Jon Jackson

Classic Locked-Rooms

The Mummy Case Mystery
by Dermot Morrah

Classic Erotica

The Ups & Downs of Life
by Capt. Edward Sellon

Literature

Whores by James Crumley
***Everybody's* Metamorphosis**
by Charles Willeford

Blue Murder

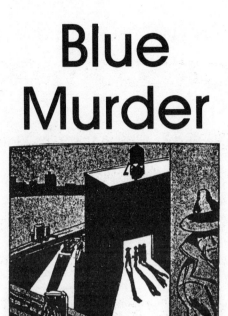

Robert Leslie Bellem

1987

Dennis McMillan Publications
1995 Calais Drive No. 3
Miami Beach, Florida 33141

Introduction

When Edgar Allan Poe wrote the first detective stories in the 1840's, he could not possibly have envisioned the directions his new form would take in future generations. If he had known what Doyle, Chesterton, and others of similar talents would create, he might have approved. If he had known, on the other hand, that there lurked a vast horde of lurid-covered pulp magazines somewhere in the mists of time ahead, and that among those who would write for them was the awesome figure of Robert Leslie Bellem, he might have burned the manuscripts of such stories as "Murders in the Rue Morgue" and "The Purloined Letter" and run screaming into the streets.

Those of us in the modern world who have read Bellem's work might also be inclined to run screaming into the streets—but with laughter, not anguish. Anyone whose sense of humor leans toward the ribald, the outrageous, the utterly absurd is liable to find himself convulsed by Bellem's wacky, colloquial prose. The list of his admirers is long and distinguished, and includes humorist S.J. Perelman. In a *New Yorker* essay, Perelman called Bellem's immortal "private skulk," Dan Turner, "the

apotheosis of all private detectives . . . out of Ma
Barker by Dashiell Hammett's Sam Spade."

Born in 1902, Bellem began writing for the pulps
in the mid-1920's and was soon producing over a
million words a year for such magazines as *Spicy
Detective, Spicy Mystery,* and *Private Detective.* In
1942, he helped launch his own magazine, *Dan
Turner, Hollywood Detective* (later *Hollywood Detective*),
which featured at least one and sometimes several Turner capers. In less than three decades, Bellem penned the staggering total of 3,000 pulp stories.
He also found time to write two novels under his own
name, two collaborative novels with Cleve F. Adams,
and a ghosted mystery. When the pulp market col-
lapsed in the early '50's, he concentrated on teleplays
and was a regular contributor to such popular TV
shows as *The Lone Ranger, Superman,* and *Perry
Mason.*

None of Bellem's novels feature Dan Turner—no
doubt because his style was at its most hilariously
nutty in the Turner stories, and while pulp readers
gobbled it up, book publishers of the time surely
found it *too* bizarre for the lending library trade. For
instance: "A thunderous bellow flashed from Dave
Donaldson's service .38, full at the prop man's elly-
bay. Welch gasped like a leaky flue, hugged his
punctured tripes, and slowly doubled over, fell flat
on his smeller." And: "From the window . . . a roscoe
sneezed: *Ka-chee!* and a red-hot hornet creased its
stinger across my dome, bashed me to dreamland."

Bellem did, however, create another tough, wise-
cracking private eye for his first novel, *Blue Murder,*
originally published by Phoenix Press in 1938. Duke
Pizzatello may not be quite as screwball a character

as Dan Turner, but he resembles Turner closely enough to be his brother. And if Bellem toned down his style a bit for the telling of the Duke's only case, he certainly didn't resort to a solemn or mundane prose style. The wacky flavor of his Dan Turner pulp romps is very much in evidence in these pages, as witness such passages as: "I aimed my own roscoe from the hip. It said: 'Chow-chow!' and belched two slugs through Mason's right leg. The slugs kicked his gam from under him, and he spun around and sat down on the floor and got a silly look on his hard-boiled pan . . ."

This reissue of *Blue Murder* is an event, one guaranteed to please all fans of Bellem, Dan Turner, pulp-style fiction, and the kind of *reductio ad absurdum* story that makes you laugh out loud.

Was Bellem's tongue firmly planted in his cheek when he chronicled the adventures of his various private skulks and other pulp heroes? Or was he a "serious" writer who had little or no idea of the comic absurdity of his style? There has been much debate about this, but no one seems to know for sure. Certain conclusions can be drawn, however, from anecdotes such as the following related by Western pulp writer Frank Bonham, who knew Bellem reasonably well in the '40's and '50's.

"The first time my wife and I were invited to the Bellem house for dinner," Bonham recalls, "we found a baby's highchair placed at the dining room table. This seemed odd because we knew Bellem and his wife, B.B., were childless. Just as we were about to sit down, Bellem produced a large, somewhat seedy toy panda bear and put it in the highchair. This was no joke; he acted as though it were a nightly ritual—

which it was, as we later found out. He introduced
the stuffed animal as "Bear," B.B. set a plate of fresh
eucalyptus leaves in front of it, and we all proceeded
to eat a very quiet dinner."

They don't make writers like Robert Leslie Bellem
anymore, folks. Nor do writers make detectives like
Dan Turner and Duke Pizzatello anymore, either.

Dammit.

Bill Pronzini
Sonoma, California
April 1987

One

I WALKED INTO THE OFFICE and sat down at my desk and pulled out a lower drawer to rest my feet on while I lit a cigarette.

Dixie Parker saw me. Dixie was private secretary to Steve Kohlar, one of my two detective agency bosses. She got up from her typewriter and came toward me, rolling her hips and patting back her yellow hair.

She leaned over me and smiled. Her dress was cut plenty low in front, and her skin was white and creamy. I took a good look and said: "Hi, babe. Remind me to buy you a brassiere for Christmas."

"Nuts, you Dago louse," she flipped back at me, without getting sore. "Remind me to buy you a set of blinkers." Then she said: "Kohlar told me he wanted to talk to you as soon as you got in, Duke."

I said: "Steve or Joe?"

"Steve."

I patted Dixie on the thigh and said: "Okay, babe." I was glad it was Steve Kohlar that wanted to see me instead of his younger brother and partner, Joe. It made me jittery here lately to talk to Joe. I guess maybe it was my conscience.

I got up and walked over to the door of Steve Kohlar's private office. I knocked, and Steve's voice rumbled: "Come in."

I opened the door. Steve was sitting at his desk, chewing a black cigar. "You wanted to see me, boss?" I asked him.

He said: "Yeah. I got a job for you. A divorce job."

I said: "Divorce job? Wait a minute, boss. I'm no good on divorce stuff."

"You're the only man I can spare for this case just now, Duke. You can handle it all right."

I was just about to put up some more belly ache when I heard a noise in Steve's private can, and the door opened and a dame walked out into the office.

She was a tall, red-haired bimbo with green eyes—like a cat. She moved like a cat, too—slinky, without making any noise. She had a million-dollar shape, with plenty of curves—all in the right places. Her hips rippled with every step she took. Her dress looked as if it might be glued on her.

Steve said: "Mrs. Mason, this is my ace operative, Duke Pizzatello."

The dame smiled at me and said: "How do you do, Mr. Pizzatello?" in a voice that purred and had fur on it.

"Hello," I said. I crushed out my cigarette.

Steve said: "You can trust Pizzatello with the whole story Mrs. Mason. Suppose you let him drive you home, and you can tell him about it on the way."

"All right, Mr. Kohlar," she said.

He helped her on with her mink coat. Then she put her hand in the crook of my elbow and smiled at me again and we went out together. We walked down to my coupé parked on the corner.

Mrs. Mason sat plenty close to me. I didn't mind that a bit, because she had plenty on the ball and I got a kick out of feeling her next to me. I gunned past a traffic light just as it turned from amber to red. Mrs. Mason said: "Are you handy with a camera and flashlight, Mr. Pizzatello?"

"Not very."

"That's funny. Mr. Kohlar told me you were the best private detective on his staff."

"Yeah. But I just work on insurance cases and robberies and things like that. Divorce evidence stuff if out of my line."

"I see." She got quiet for a while. Then she said: "Have you ever shot anybody, Mr. Pizzatello? I mean, have you ever killed anyone?"

I gave her a quick look out of the tail of my eyes. Her face was sort of set and grim. I wondered what the hell she was getting at. I said: "Yeah. I've killed three guys. But it was in the course of duty—after they cut loose on me first. Why?"

She inched even closer to me. "Would you consider shooting a man for money?"

I said: "Look. I'm a detective, not an assassin. If I have to rub out a guy in the line of duty, that's one thing. But I wouldn't hire out to croak anybody in cold blood. I'm no hood."

She laughed deep down in her white throat, but it didn't sound very convincing. "I was just teasing you, Mr. Pizzatello. Just to see what you'd say."

I didn't know whether to believe her or not. There was something cold and vindictive about her at that instant. She acted like a dame who wouldn't hesitate to jam a shiv into the ribs of somebody she didn't like. She sort of gave me the creeps. But she made me feel all warm and funny inside, too, sitting so close to me that way. Maybe it was the perfume she wore.

I kept on driving. Pretty soon she said: "You're going to help me get a divorce from my husband, aren't you?"

"I don't know. It all depends on what you want me to do."

"You won't have to do much. Just catch him with the woman he's chasing around with. Take a picture of them together. A compromising picture."

"I don't much like that kind of work," I told her.

She said: "But I know you'll help me when I explain things to you." Then she pointed to a house. "Here's where I live. Come inside so we can talk."

I stopped my jaloppy at the curb and Mrs. Mason took me into the house. She took off her coat and hat and left me while she went to pour a couple of drinks. Then she came back and sat down alongside me on the chaise longue. She said: "What's your first name, Mr. Pizzatello?"

"Everybody calls me Duke."

"Well, then, I'll call you Duke, too. And you can call me Nelia if you want to."

"Okay, Nelia," I said.

She raised her glass. "Here's to crime, Duke."

I didn't answer. I just drank. It was good rye.

She put down her empty glass and said: "Do you happen to know my husband, Duke?"

"No."

"He's Dr. Carney Mason. He's a rat."

"Is he?"

"Yes. I've been married to him ten years. Ten years of pure hell."

"You mean because he bats around with other dames?"

"Not only that, Duke. There are other reasons. Wait here a minute and I'll show you a few." She got up and left me and went upstairs. After a while she came back down again. She had taken off her dress, and she was wearing a thin negligee with nothing underneath—as far as I could discover.

She dropped the negligee down over her shoulders, baring the upper halves of her lush white breasts. "Look, Duke," she said.

I looked. Her arms and shoulders were all black and blue.

I touched the bruises. There was something about the feel of her naked flesh that made my fingers tingle. She let the front of her negligee come open pretty far. I could see plenty of interesting things under the thin silk.

But I kept my mind on her black and blue marks. I said: "Your husband biff you, Nelia?"

"Yes. He's always beating me."

"Looks like that ought to be enough for a divorce, without having to catch him with some broad."

"It ought to be, but is isn't. After all, he never hits me before witnesses. He isn't that dumb. If I dragged him into court, he'd swear I put the bruises on myself to frame him."

"Oh. You think he'd fight a divorce action, huh?"

"Yes. That's why I need you to get the goods on him, Duke. Don't you understand?" She slipped her negligee open a little more.

I said: "Yeah. I'm beginning to get the lay now."

"And you'll help me?"

I started to nod. At the same time, I thought I heard a sound behind me, like a door opening and closing again. Then, before I knew what it was all about, Nelia Mason threw herself at me.

She slipped all the way out of the negligee, and I saw she wasn't wearing anything else except skintight pink panties. She put her bare arms around my neck, and I felt her breasts jabbing into my chest like a couple of firm torpedoes. She fastened her open mouth against mine.

I was plenty startled. I wasn't expecting her to act that way. I tried to back off.

And then, from behind me, a man's voice said: "You wife-stealing son of a bitch!"

Two

I WAS ON MY TOES and had my roscoe out of its shoulder-holster all in one move. Nelia Mason screamed: *"Carney!"*

I saw her husband standing in the doorway of the room. He was a chunky-built guy with shoulders like an ape and hairy hands, and in his left hand he had a big automatic.

He was aiming the automatic at my belly-button and squeezing the trigger and cursing because no bullets were coming out of his rod. He had forgotten to unlatch the safety.

I aimed my own roscoe from the hip. It said: *"Chow-chow!"* and belched two slugs through Mason's right leg. The slugs kicked his gam from under him, and he spun around and sat down on the floor and got a silly look on his hard-boiled pan.

Nelia Mason screamed again. "You've killed him!"

I slapped her across the kisser, hard. "Shut up!" I said. Then I grabbed my hat and lammed through the doorway. I knew I hadn't bumped her husband. I'd just crippled him a little. I got out of the house and jumped into my jaloppy and drove like all hell.

I thought I could see the whole damned set-up, and it smelled plenty bad. Nelia Mason had wanted her old man croaked. She had probably expected him home at this particular hour, so she had deliberately trapped me into a compromising pose with her. She must have figured the doctor would discover us together and go for his rod. But she had also doped it out that I would be faster on the draw and pump a few chunks of lead through his intestines.

Well, I had fooled her. I had just wounded Mason, instead of knocking him off. But even that was bad enough. If he ever decided to come after me with the law, I would be holding the red-hot end of the poker.

Of course there was one thing in my favor. Mason didn't know me from Adam. I'd even grabbed my hat when I tore out of his house, so he couldn't trace me that way. But I was in a ticklish spot just the same. If Mason did happen to trace me, I would be up Brown Creek without any oars. I didn't like any part of it.

I drove to my apartment and put my coupé away in the basement garage and hoped to God nobody had tabbed my license number. I went upstairs to my flat and unlocked the door and walked in. It was just dusk.

Somebody said: "Hello, Duke."

I jumped and swore and snapped on the lights. "Gertie!" I whispered.

It was Gertie Kohlar, wife of Joe Kohlar, the junior partner in the detective agency where I worked. She was a cuddly little brunette, with all the sex appeal in the world. She was wearing a knit dress that stuck to her like poured oil, and when she walked toward me she jiggled up and down, cuter than hell. She was an eye-full.

I said: "What in God's name are you doing here, Gertie? How did you get in?"

"I got the porter to let me in. I had to see you, Duke."

"What about?"

"Ain't you gonna kiss me first?" she pouted.

I said: "Wait a minute, Gertie. That stuff is out. I told you that long ago. And besides, suppose Joe trailed you here? What would he think?"

"You needn't worry about Joe. He ain't wise. He don't suspect we been playing around together."

I said: "Where do you get that playing around stuff, Gertie? Just because I happened to run into you on a party one night, and we both got a little fried and forgot ourselves—"

She narrowed her eyes. "That one night was plenty, Duke. That's what I want to talk to you about."

"Yeah," I said. "You been wanting to talk about it ever since it happened. I keep telling you we were both crazy that night, Gertie. Jesus, anybody can slip off the straight and narrow once in a while. But it don't have to go on forever."

"Oh, no?"

"No. Now run along, Gertie. Try and understand the way things are. You're married. Your husband is one of my bosses. You and I got pickled one night and sort of lost control. Well, what happened is all over and done with. Let's forget about it and just be good friends, the way we used to be. It gives me the screaming meemies to have you here in my joint, and I'm nervous enough to begin with."

"What are you nervous about?"

"I'm nervous on account of something that just happened to me," I told her. "A dame hired me to get divorce evidence against her husband. Then she framed me into a spot where I had to put a couple of slugs through his leg. I think she wanted me to kill him, but I didn't. I just crippled him a little; then I lammed. The whole thing has got me jittery."

Gertie said: "I don't see why you should be jittery over shootin' a guy. It ain't the first time. You already got three notches on your gun."

"Yeah. But it was self-defense every time. And besides, today was different. This guy's wife actually wanted him croaked, the way I figure. She tried to put him on the spot and make me the fall guy. At the very start, she hinted about paying me dough to bump him."

"How much dough?"

"I don't know. I didn't ask. I'm not a murderer."

Gertie said: "Well, boy-friend, you better go back and find out how much the dame will give you to finish what you started. I'm tellin' you."

I looked at her. "What the hell you getting at?"

"I mean we're gonna need some cash pretty quick, Duke."

"We? Who you mean: 'we'?"

"I mean you and me."

I said: "I don't get you, Gertie."

She walked up close to me. "You're gonna need at least three hundred berries to give me so I can go away somewhere and have an operation without Joe findin' out about it."

"An operation?"

"Yeah. You know what kind."

I stared at her. "You mean you're—?"

"Yeah. That's exactly what I do mean. And it's gonna cost you at least three hundred clams."

"So you're blaming it on me, huh?"

"Who else would I blame it on, damn your Wop eyes? If you think I been runnin' around with anybody else—"

"No, I didn't say that."

"You better not. You know I don't play around, Duke. I never played around with any man—only once. That one night with you."

I said: "Okay. I'll take your word for it. But why drag me into the mess? Can't you blame it on Joe? After all, he's your husband."

She laughed. "That's a joke. You know Joe was wounded in the war. Wouldn't it be sweet, me goin' to him and tellin' him what's wrong with me, when he knows the shape he's in?"

"Christ," I said.

Gertie said: "Well, what about it? You got three hundred fish to slip me right now?"

"Hell, no. I haven't got twenty bucks to rub together. I never have any dough from one pay day to the next. The dice eat me up. You know that."

"Well, I gotta have at last three hundred bucks, Duke. You gotta get it for me some way."

"Why three hundred? The regular price is fifty, I always thought."

"Yeah? You want me to stay here in town and have Joe find out? Not on your tintype! I gotta have money to take a trip somewhere. I'll tell Joe I'm goin' to visit my sister in Chi. Then I'll sneak to some town close by, and everything will be okay."

I said: "All right, Gertie. I'll see what I can do."

"Well, do it quick, or else pretty soon Joe will start askin' me questions."

"Okay. Now beat it and let me think."

"You seem in an awful hurry to get rid of me. You got some broad comin' here tonight?"

"No. Of course not."

"All right, then, you Dago dope. Come on. Loosen up and kiss me."

I figured the quickest way to get rid of her was to do what she wanted, so I kissed her. She pressed herself up against me, and I could feel the warmth of her body as she snuggled up close to my chest. Gertie Kohlar didn't have much book learning, but she knew a lot of things they don't teach in grammar school. When I put my arms around her, she quivered all over, and I had a hell of a time persuading her to leave.

When she was gone, I had three quick snorts of rye to steady my nerves, and then I started to go out. Just as I made for the door, the phone rang. I picked it up and said: "Hello."

"Is that you, Duke?"

"Yeah."

"This is Dixie Parker."

I wondered what the hell Steve Kohlar's secretary wanted with me. I said: "Hi, babe. What's on your mind?"

"Plenty. Can you come over to my flat right away? I want to talk to you."

"What about? Can't you spill it over the phone?"

"No, I can't."

"Well, then, won't it wait till morning?"

"It won't. It's important, Duke. Important to you."

"Okay. I'll come right over, babe."

"I'll be waiting."

I hung up and went downstairs to the basement and got into my jaloppy and drove over to where Dixie lived. I went up to her flat and knocked on the door and she let me in.

She was wearing green silk pajamas you could see through. She closed the door and walked toward me, rolling her hips and patting her yellow hair. "Hello, Wop."

"Hello, babe. I still think you need a brassiere for Christmas."

"Never mind that. I want to tell you something."

"Okay. Give."

"It's about that red-haired woman in Steve Kohlar's office this afternoon. The one you went out with. What did she want you to do for her?"

"Nothing much. Get divorce evidence against her husband."

"That was all, Duke? On the level?"

I couldn't see any use telling Dixie how I'd almost been framed into a bump-off job. "On the level," I said.

"Well, listen to me. I like you, Wop. And I've got a hunch that woman is going to get you in a jam. Steer clear of her."

"You been crystal-gazing?"

Dixie said: "No. Just feminine intuition." She came up

close to me, so I could smell the perfume of her yellow
hair. "Promise me you'll lay off that dame, Duke."

"I'll think it over."

"No. I want a promise. Listen, big boy. You're going out
to see her tonight, aren't you?"

"Never even gave it a thought," I lied.

"I don't believe you. Anyhow, I don't want you to go.
Stay here with me instead."

I looked at her. She was a sweet dish, all right, in that
peek-a-boo pajama outfit. When she stood in front of a
light, she might just as well have been naked. I began to
think maybe it would be nice to stay and visit with her
for awhile.

Then I thought of Gertie Kohlar, who needed ready
cash on account of me. The only way I could lay my hands
on some quick dough was to do business with Nelia Mason.
I don't mean I was going to tell Mrs. Mason I'd be willing
to croak her husband for money. But maybe I could talk
her into forking over some advance jack if I agreed to get
divorce evidence against him, as soon as he got over those
two slugs I'd planted in his leg.

So I said: "Dixie, you're a sweet kid. But I've got to go
out tonight."

"You mean you're not interested in staying here with
me?"

"I'm plenty interested, babe. You've got what it takes.
But I can't stay." I slipped an arm around her waist and
kissed her on the mouth and patted her hips a little. "So
long, babe."

"You Dago fool!" she whispered. She pushed away from
me.

I grinned at her and went out. But when I got downstairs to my coupé, the night seemed mighty damned dark
all of a sudden.

Three

I DROVE OUT to the suburbs, where Steve Kohlar lived with his brother Joe and Joe's wife, Gertie. They shared a bungalow on a side street, and there was a light in the front room when I parked outside.

I went up on the porch and rang the bell. The front door opened and Joe Kohlar stood there looking at me. Joe had funny, washed-out blue eyes, and lately, whenever he turned them on me, I felt jumpy. That was because of what had happened between me and his wife. I didn't think he suspected me of anything, but just the same he made me nervous. If he ever found out I had made love to Gertie that one night, there was no telling what he might do. He had a nasty temper and a quick trigger-finger.

He seemed a little surprised to see me standing there on the porch. He said: "Hello, Duke. What's on your mind?"

I said: "Is Steve in, Joe? I'd like to see him."

"Yes, he's here. Come on in. I'll call him."

I went into the living room. Gertie was sitting in a big chair, reading a magazine. She gave me a polite nod and said: "How do you do, Mr. Pizzatello"—very formal. To hear her, nobody would ever have guessed that she'd been in my apartment not long before, kissing me.

Joe went to the back of the house, and pretty soon Steve walked in. He said: "Well, Duke?"

"Listen, boss," I said, "I'd like to talk to you in private. How about getting in my jalopy and riding around the block?"

"Sure."

We went out and I drove around for awhile. I said: "Boss, about that Mason dame. I plugged her husband this afternoon. Twice. Through the leg."

"Yeah. She phoned me and told me."

"Well, did she tell you how she framed the whole damned mess? That wren didn't want any divorce, Steve. She wanted me to croak the doctor. That's the way it stacks up to me. She fixed things so he'd walk in and find her in my arms and go for his roscoe. I had to shoot him in self-defense."

Steve grunted. "I think you've got her all wrong. If you ask me, the whole thing was an accident, from the way she explained it to me over the phone."

"Yeah? Well, it might have been a damned bad accident. I might have got a slug through my own belly if Mason hadn't forgot to unlatch the safety on his rod. And if I hadn't aimed low, I might have cooled him off plenty."

Steve said: "Well, as long as you didn't, what are you worrying about?"

"Plenty," I came back. "I suppose I'm in Dutch with the law now. Mason has probably put in a beef to the cops."

"No. He didn't squawk. Mrs. Mason told me over the phone that he didn't want to report the shooting for fear it might make a newspaper scandal and maybe damage his professional prestige. And besides, your bullets didn't hurt him."

"Didn't hurt him?"

"No." Steve grinned at me. "You didn't know it, but Mason's got a game leg. Artificial from the knee down. Your slugs hit his cork gam."

I felt as if somebody had lifted a ton of grief off my shoulders. "Jesus, that's a break!" I said.

"You said it."

"Well, look, boss. If that's the way things are, maybe

Mrs. Mason will still want to hire me to get divorce evidence for her, huh?"

Kohlar said: "Maybe. Why?"

"Well, if she does, I'd like to work on the case for her."

"I thought you didn't like divorce cases."

"I don't. But I need some quick geetus."

"Well, I'll see about it. I'll phone her and ask her if she still craves your services. You go on home and wait."

"Okay. Thanks, boss." I let him out in front of his house, and then drove back to my flat and went upstairs. I had a couple of snorts of rye, and then I took out the clip of my roscoe and filled it.

I waited maybe two hours, and then the phone rang. I unforked the receiver and said: "Hello?"

"This is Nelia Mason, Duke. Are you alone?"

"Yeah."

"I'll be right over to your place."

"Okay. I'm waiting."

I hung up and had a couple more drinks, and pretty soon there was a knock at my door. I opened it and Nelia Mason walked in. She had a close-fitting hat pulled over her red hair and a short veil on her face. She was wearing a dark coat which she didn't take off when she sat down.

She crossed her legs, and I caught a glimpse of pink garters and white skin and stain step-ins. But I didn't get steamed up over what I saw, because the last time I'd got heated up over Nelia Mason I'd had to shoot my way out of a jam.

When she saw I wasn't interested in her legs, she pulled her skirt down and said: "Your boss phoned me, Duke. He told me you'd help me get my divorce evidence, after all."

"Yeah. I'll do it. But how about advancing me some money first? Say three hundred berries."

She looked me square in the eye and said: "You get a flashlight picture of my husband and his mistress together, and I'll pay you twice as much."

"Okay; that suits me. The question is: when and where do I catch him with his broad?"

"You'll find him at his office downtown, in the Medico-Surgical Court. He's there now, and he's got his lady friend with him."

I went and got my candid camera and saw that it was loaded with films. I fixed up my flashlight dingus and put it in my pocket and turned to Nelia Mason. "Let's go, lady."

We went down and got into my coupé and I drove downtown. I said: "How come you're so sure we'll catch the doctor in his office?"

"Because, after you shot him in his artificial leg this afternoon, he got up and ran after you, but you'd got away. Then he came back into the house and cursed me and hit me and started drinking. After that I heard him phoning his girl friend to meet him at his office tonight, and then he went out. So I'm sure he's got a date with her."

Just then I swung into Madison Street, where the Medico-Surgical Court was located. As I tooled my jaloppy around the corner, a big limousine cut in front of me, coming out of Madison, and I almost ploughed into it. I swerved my wheel hard, and my headlights spotted the limousine's chauffeur. He was a tough-looking egg with a funny white scar across his cheek, and there was a thin little grey-haired dame sitting in the back seat, staring straight ahead.

Alongside me, Nelia Mason stiffened and sort of ducked down. "I know that woman! I hope she didn't see me!"

I said: "It's okay. My lights were directly on her. She couldn't see past the glare. Why don't you want her to see you?"

"No reason."

By that time the limousine was gone, and I finished turning into Madison, and pretty soon I parked at the curb. The Medico-Surgical Court was a bunch of bun-

galows arranged in a sort of U-shape fronting on Madison,
all occupied by doctors. All the bungalows were dark.

Mrs. Mason handed me a key. "It's the last cottage at
the rear of the court. This key will let you in the back
door. There's a waiting room in front, then an office. Behind the office there are two surgeries. One belongs to Dr.
Sebring, my husband's medical partner. The other surgery
is my husband's. That's where you'll probably find him
with his mistress. They usually spend their evenings in
there together. An operating table can be used for more
things than operations!"

I took the key and swung my camera around in front
of me on its leather strap. Then I left Mrs. Mason sitting
in my coupé while I started for the rear of the medical
court.

There weren't any pedestrians on the street, and nobody saw me sneaking along the flagstone path in the
darkness. I reached the last bungalow and edged up close
to a sign on its front. The sign read:

DR. CARNEY MASON
DR. WILLOUGHBY SEBRING
Physicians—Surgeons
Office Hours, 1 P.M. to 4:30 P.M.
Saturdays by Appointment

So I knew I was at the right place. I walked around on
my tiptoes to the rear of the bungalow and came to a door.
I tried the key Nelia Mason had given me.

It worked. The door opened. I slipped inside. Everything
was dark as hell, except for a little gleam of very dim
yellow light trickling around the edges of a closed door on
the other side of the room.

I got out my flashlight bulb and opened the lens of my

camera and wound up the shutter. Then I went to the closed door, where the light leaked through, and kicked it open with my foot and raised my camera.

I said: "Oh, Christ—!"

There was a night light burning in one corner of that surgery. In front of me, I saw a couch. Dr. Carney Mason was lying on the couch, with his eyes open, staring up at the ceiling without seeing it. He'd never see anything again. There was a blue hole in his left temple where a bullet had gone in, and another jagged red hole in the right temple where it had come out. His brains had spewed out of that second hole, and he was as dead as Napoleon.

But that wasn't what got me. The thing that churned my belly was on the operating table in the center of the surgery. It was a dead, naked dame. Or rather, it was something that had been a dame, a while ago. Now it was nothing but a carved-up piece of meat.

Four

FOR A MINUTE I thought I was going to heave up my toenails. There was blood everywhere, and you couldn't tell a damned thing about the dame who had been croaked. Somebody had cut her throat, and then wiped out every possible means of identifying her.

First she had been scalped with a sharp knife, leaving nothing but the glistening raw skull with shreds of flesh clinging to it. There wasn't a hair left on her to show whether she had been blonde, brunette or red-haired. A scalpel had gouged out her eyeballs so you couldn't guess what color her eyes had been.

All the flesh had been sliced away from her face, and her teeth had been knocked out with a chisel, evidently. The hands had been worked on, too. The finger-tips were all messed up, leaving no chance for taking fingerprints.

I didn't see all that stuff at first, because the light was too dim. But, after I got over the first shock, I took a long chance and found the light-switch and flipped it on, and a big electric dome-light over the operating table threw a glaring white light down on that mutilated female cadaver.

My first thought was that Mason had bumped the dame and carved her up and then shot himself through the head. But, when I took another look at him on the cot, I knew I was wrong, because there wasn't any roscoe in his hand or on the floor alongside him. And there wasn't any blood on his corpse, whereas, if he had killed the dame, he would have been red from head to foot, the way her juice had spewed out.

So then I realized that someone had come in here and croaked the doctor and his lady friend and then lammed. All of a sudden it struck me I'd better be getting the hell out of there before somebody found me with those two stiffs.

My knees were knocking together like Spanish castanets, and my belly was churning, and my hands were cold and sweaty, and my tongue felt dry and thick, as if I'd been eating glue.

I got a grip on myself and started for the door. The inner knob felt gummy and sticky to my fingers, and I knew I had touched blood. Then, just as I stepped out of the surgery, I heard footsteps coming toward me from the waiting room at the front of the bungalow.

I thought it was Nelia Mason, and I said: "Don't come in here, for Christ's sake!"

But the footsteps kept coming, slow and heavy, and then a voice said: "Stick up your hands!"

I snatched my rod out of its shoulder-holster and whirled around. I saw a blue-uniformed copper walking toward me with his service .38 in his fist.

My guts froze up tight. I knew I was in a spot. I saw the copper stare past me into that surgery, and, when he got a gander at the two corpses, he let out a grunt and dived at me.

I tried to duck him, but my legs seemed paralyzed. He snatched my roscoe out of my hand and jammed his own rod into my belly and said: "Damned lucky thing I noticed the light in here and came in to investigate!"

I said: "Listen, officer, I didn't—"

"I suppose you're gonna try and tell me you don't know nothin' about them two stiffs, huh?"

"No, I don't. Honest to God, I just came in here and found them—"

"Shut up. If you got anything to say, save it for your lawyer."

"But those stiffs are cold!" I said. "They been dead an hour or more. I can prove I just came in here a couple of minutes ago."

"I ain't askin' you to prove nothin'. Stick out your mitts for the bracelets."

I was thinking fast. My only way was to get hold of Nelia Mason and have her back up my story that I had just entered the bungalow. I said: "Look, officer. There's a lady outside who'll tell you I just came in here. I'm not lying. You don't think I'd lie in a spot like this, do you?"

"There ain't no lady outside. I walked in the front way, and I didn't see no lady."

"Maybe she's sitting in my coupé, that's parked at the curb. That's where I left her."

"There ain't no coupé parked at the curb. There ain't no cars parked on this block at all. Now stick out your fins. Or would you rather have me sock you over the noggin with my rod?"

I felt weak. If my coupé wasn't at the curb, then Nelia Mason must have driven it away and left me in the lurch. "The dirty bitch!" I whispered.

The copper grabbed for my right wrist, and that's when I got a break. When he grabbed for me, his foot slipped in the blood on the floor and he sort of went off balance.

I brought up my left fist and bopped him in the kisser. He staggered, and I hit him again, and he went down. I snatched my automatic back out of his hand as he fell; then I leaped over him and raced for the door of the bungalow. I hit the door with my right shoulder, and it smashed open, and I went flying out into the night.

I couldn't see anybody around the front of the court. My jaloppy wasn't at the curb, and Nelia Mason was gone. So the harness bull had told me the truth about that. I cursed Mrs. Mason for ditching me when I needed her most, and I started running up the street.

As I ran, I dragged out my handkerchief and wiped the
blood off my hand where I had touched that surgery door-
knob, and then I threw the handkerchief in the gutter
and kept on going. When I got near Colorado Street, which
is the main stem, I slowed down to a fast walk. There was
a Yellow drifting past with its flag up.

I hailed it and jumped in. "Arroyo Drive," I told the
driver, and I gave him Steve Kohlar's address.

The cab lurched forward, and I huddled back in the
seat and had a fit of the creeping trembles. I kept looking
back through the rear window of the cab to see if I was
being tailed, but, as far as I could tell, I wasn't being. The
drive to the Kohlar place seemed to last about five hours.
But pretty soon we got there and I got out of the Yellow
and paid the cabby; and as soon as he drifted away, I ran
up on the porch and rang hell out of the doorbell.

After a while, the door opened and Steve Kohlar himself
let me in. I didn't see any sign of his brother, Joe. Steve
looked at me and said: "Pizzatello—what the hell's wrong,
man? You look white as a goddam sheet!"

"Listen, boss. Something's happened. Something
screwy. I'm in a jam. You got to get me out of it."

"A jam?"

"Yeah. A bad one."

"What kind of a jam?"

"A murder rap, boss."

"Murder? Good God! Who did you croak?"

"I didn't croak anybody. But Dr. Mason's been rubbed
out in his surgery. An there's a dead dame with him, all
carved up. A cop caught me in Mason's bungalow-office,
but I managed to get away."

Steve said: "Better keep your voice down, Pizzatello.
We'll go outside to talk this over. Wait a minute till I go
back and leave a message for Joe."

He left me there in his living room and went to the
back part of the house. I heard him saying: "Listen, Gertie.

When Joe comes in, tell him to stick around and not to go out again. I'm going on an errand, and I want to see him as soon as I get back."

"Okay, Steve. I'll tell him." That was Gertie's voice.

Then Steve came back into the living room and we went out of the house together. He got his car out of the garage at the rear, and I got in alongside him, and he started to drive nowhere in particular. He said: "Now, tell me everything that happened."

So I spilled the works to him. When I got through, he looked at me and said: "Duke, you're in a hell of a fix—and I don't mean maybe!"

Five

I FELT LIKE SAYING: "Yeah, and it's all on account of your brother's wife. If Gertie hadn't put the sting on me for dough, I wouldn't have let Nelia Mason drag me into this mess!"

But of course I didn't say anything like that. Instead, I said: "What do you figure I ought to do, boss—lam out of town?"

"No. Not yet. The best thing for you to do is to go home to your flat and lay low until I see what can be done."

"You got any angles, boss?"

Steve looked at me. "Maybe—provided you've told me the truth. Listen, you haven't lied to me, have you?"

"Lied to you, boss? What about?"

"I mean—you're really on the level about being in that bungalow just a couple of minutes?"

"God, yes! Jesus—you don't really think I croaked Mason and that broad, do you?"

He thought a minute, and then said: "Well, no; I don't think you did it. In the first place, you wouldn't have any motive."

I felt better when he said that. "Then you'll help me?" I asked him.

"Yeah. The first thing I'll probably do is get in touch with Mrs. Mason. She's your alibi."

"Alibi—hell!" I said. "She's probably the murderer! That's why she lammed away and left me holding the bag. She did the killing, and then sucked me into a frame-up, thinking I'd have to take the rap for her."

"You may be right," Steve said. "But, just the same, she's the only one who knows you weren't in that medical bungalow long enough to carve up that dame and croak the doctor. If she's innocent, she'll front for you. If she's guilty, she'll refuse. And that alone will give us something to go on. We can start using her as our main suspect."

His reasoning sounded plenty good to me. I began to feel a little easier in my mind. I told him so.

He said: "Don't let yourself get too chipper. You're not out of the woods yet, by a hell of a sight. And now I'll drive you to your apartment, and you can hole up until I get in touch with you."

He drove me to my place, and I got out of his car, and the first thing I saw was my own jaloppy parked at the curb. I said: "Look, boss—here's my heap! Mrs. Mason must have brought it here and left it after she took that powder on me downtown."

"Yeah," Steve said. "Well, put it in your garage and go on upstairs and wait for me to phone you."

He drove off and left me standing there. I climbed into my coupé and put it in the basement garage, and then I went upstairs to my flat and let myself in. There was a light burning in my living room, and I didn't remember leaving it turned on. I began to feel funny.

Then I heard the faucet running in my bathroom. The bathroom door opened, and somebody walked out and said: "Hello, Wop."

It was Dixie Parker. I stared at her. "How the hell did you get in here, babe? How long you been here?"

"I picked your lock with a hairpin. I've been here all evening. Ever since you left me at my place."

"You been waiting here ever since then? How come?"

"Because I've still got my hunch you're headed for trouble, Wop."

"Trouble? God almighty, I've already got all the trouble there ever was!"

"What do you mean?"

"I mean you were right about that red-haired Mason jane. She got me in one God-awful mess."

"What kind of mess?"

I told Dixie everything that had happened. When I got finished, her face was white and scared-looking. She said: "Duke—you didn't really do the killing, did you?"

"No. So help me God, I didn't do it."

"But you'll be arrested for it, won't you?"

"I suppose I will, if the cops trace me. But I don't see how they can. I got my roscoe back from that harness bull. There's no other way he can track me down—I hope!"

"But suppose they do trace you, Duke? They'll try to break you and make you confess you were the murderer!"

"They can't make me confess something I didn't do, babe."

"But they'll third-degree you, Wop. They'll beat you up and torture you and try to make you talk!"

"They got to find me first," I grinned. Just as I said it, I heard heavy footsteps outside my apartment door.

Somebody pounded hell out of the door and shouted: "Open up. The law!"

"Christ!" I whispered.

Dixie grabbed me. "Hurry. Into the bedroom, Duke! Listen—give me your camera and flashlight!"

"What you want it for?"

"Never mind. Quick—give!"

I handed her my candid camera and the flash-bulb dingus from my pocket, and we went into my bedroom. Dixie said: "Strip, Duke! Fast!"

I didn't know what she had on her mind, but I figured it was plenty important. The coppers were beginning to pound on my front door again. I peeled down to my shorts. Dixie handed me a late edition of that evening's newspaper. "Hold this to your waist so the headline and date will show!"

I held it the way she said. She aimed the camera at me, and cut loose the flash-bulb and took my picture. Then she stuffed the camera under the bed and started getting herself undressed in a hell of a hurry.

I watched her. She shucked out of her dress, and she wasn't wearing anything else except a mesh bandeau over her breasts and silk panties on her hips. Her skin was like snow, only a lot warmer looking. I'd never seen a prettier pair of thighs.

She kicked off her shoes and dived into my bed and pulled the covers up over her. Then I heard my front door being busted down, and all of a sudden three uniformed coppers came tearing into the bedroom with their gats in their hands. One of the bulls said: "Get 'em up, Pizzatello."

I put up my hands and said: "What's the idea?"

"You know goddam well what the idea is. You croaked Dr. Mason tonight, and bumped the dame he had with him in his office. Then you slugged the officer that arrested you, and got away. But you dropped a bloody handkerchief in the gutter outside that medical court, and we traced you by its laundry-mark."

"Listen. You got me all wrong," I said. "I never croaked—"

"Shut up and get dressed!" One of the cops saw my clothes on the floor and my roscoe in its shoulder-harness. He picked up the rod and grinned at me. "The medical examiner pried two slugs out of Dr. Mason's cork leg a while ago. I'm betting them slugs match up with the rifling in this gat of yours!"

I felt my heart turn a flip-flop. "Listen. I admit I put two bullets in Mason's game leg, but that was this afternoon. The slug that killed him went through his brain and, if you find it, you'll see it won't match up with my rod at all."

"We can't find the slug that went through his skull. But the bullets in his cork leg are enough to put your fanny in a sling."

Then Dixie Parker sat up in bed and let the covers slide down so her brassiere showed. She said: "You officers are all wet. Mr. Pizzatello hasn't been out of this apartment all evening. He and I have been right here together since supper-time."

It startled hell out of me for her to lie away her own reputation that way, just to give me a phoney alibi. I couldn't understand why she'd do it. Just then one of the harness bulls stepped forward, and I recognized him. He had a blue bruise on his jaw, and he was the copper I had slugged in making my getaway from Dr. Mason's medical bungalow.

The copper said: "Sister, you lie in your teeth. This is the guy I nabbed in Mason's surgery. Now quit tryin' to lie for him or we'll run you in too."

Dixie said: "Oh, God—"

I said: "It's okay, babe. I'll beat this rap. Steve Kohlar will help me get out of this."

The cop said: "Come on, wise guy. Climb the hell into your duds an' quit stallin'. We ain't got all night."

So I climbed the hell into my duds, and they put nippers on my wrists and took me downstairs and loaded me in a squad car and took me to the clink.

Six

THEY FINGERPRINTED ME; then they took my watch and penknife and valuables and what money I had with me. They made me strip off my clothes and take a shower bath. Then they shoved me into a cell and slammed the door on me and left me for a while.

It must have been along about midnight when they came and opened my cell and hauled me downstairs to a room full of bright lights. There was a chair in the middle of the room, and they pushed me into it. A lot of cops and plainclothes dicks stood around me, looking me over.

Then a door opened and a police captain walked in with a dame on his arm. I said: "Mrs. Mason!"

She stared back at me and never gave me a tumble. She had on her mink coat, and she looked like a million in it.

I said: "Did Steve Kohlar send you, Mrs. Mason?"

She turned to the police captain. "I don't know what he's talking about."

The captain said: "Mrs. Mason, this is the man who killed your husband. Have you ever seen him before?"

"No."

I jumped out of my chair. "Why, you goddam lying bitch!"

Somebody slugged me in the mouth and knocked me back into the chair. "Keep your filty tongue off decent women, you Dago rat."

I spat blood from my cut lips and said: "Listen. Mrs. Mason will tell you. She hired me to get divorce evidence against her husband. I'm a private dick. I work for the Kohlar Brothers' Agency—Steve and Joe Kohlar. I'm leveling with you."

Nobody paid any attention to me.

I said: "Listen, you guys. You got to listen! Mrs. Mason took me to her husband's office tonight to catch him with a dame. I walked into the office and found him dead, and the broad was dead, too—all carved up. Mrs. Mason will tell you I wasn't in there long enough to have croaked two people. Ask her. She was waiting for me outside the bungalow."

She said: "The man's lying. I never saw him before. I wasn't with him tonight at any time."

A cop looked at me and said: "Got any explanation why we found bullets from your gun in the dead man's cork leg?"

"Yes. Mrs. Mason can tell you about that, too. I was with her in her house late this afternoon. We were talking about getting her a divorce. She got undressed to show me some bruises on her arms. Then her husband walked in and caught us, and he pulled a gat on me and would have plugged me—only he forgot to unlatch the safety on his automatic. So I let him have two through the leg, in self-defense."

Mrs. Mason looked at the police captain. "Do I seem like the type who would undress in front of a rat like him?"

"No, lady. You don't. I'm sorry I had to bring you here to listen to such stuff. But we wanted to see if you could identify him as someone who had a grudge against your husband."

"No. I can't identify him. I've never seen him before, to my knowledge."

I jumped up again. "Listen, Mrs. Mason. You can't throw me down this way. You're fixing to put my neck in a length of hemp!"

She turned away. "Captain, if there's nothing else you want to ask me, I wish you'd take me home."

"Sure. Of course, Mrs. Mason. Come along." He turned to the other guys who were standing around me. "See if you can make this Dago rat talk while I'm gone."

I knew what he meant. I was going to get the third degree. I could see it coming.

Somebody arranged the lights so they flooded square in my eyes and almost blinded me. The heat beat down on my head, and I began to sweat all over.

A plainclothes dick leaned over me and said: "Listen, Pizzatello. I'm your pal—see? I'm your friend. I don't want you to get hurt, because I got a kind heart. I had a brother who looked something like you. You remind me of him. He's dead now, poor devil. I wouldn't want anything nasty to happen to you, because you remind me of my dead brother. Now why not be a good guy and tell us why you killed Dr. Mason and the dame he had with him?"

I said: "You're a goddam liar. You never had a brother, and if you did have a brother, he'd be a son of a bitch—the same as you are. And I didn't kill Mason."

"Come on, Pizzatello. Don't be like that. I tell you I'm your friend. I want to help you."

"The hell you do."

"Now look, Pizzatello. You talk to me, and I'll see if I can't help you beat this rap. Maybe you had a good reason for croaking Mason. Tell me about it."

"I've told you all I know. Lay off me."

Another plainclothes dick shoved the first one aside. "He won't listen to reason, Bill. No use being easy with him. Let me have a whack at him with the soft end of my blackjack. I'll make the bastard spill."

The first dick said: "Nix, Mike. I like this guy. He'll talk to me if I ask him to. Won't you, Pizzatello? You know I'm you're pal, don't you?"

"I know you're trying to pull a gag on me, damn you. You think you can get me to talk by being sympathetic with me. To hell with you. I don't know anything. I want a lawyer."

"A lawyer, huh?" the second dick said. He walked up to me and doubled his right fist and bashed it square against my jaw. "There's your lawyer, you bastard."

I swayed in the chair, but a lot of guys grabbed me and wouldn't let me fall. That beefy plainclothes dick hit me again, on the other side of my jaw. I felt something click and snap inside my mouth, and I felt around with my tongue and found where a molar had been knocked loose. I spat it out. It made a funny dead *tunk!* on the concrete floor when it hit. I tasted blood inside my mouth.

Then they all started working me over. I was yanked to my feet, and somebody grabbed my shirt and ripped it off me. Then three of those bastards started hitting me with their locust clubs. They biffed me over the head and they smashed the clubs down on my shoulders and back. I tried to throw up my hands to protect my face, and a blackjack took me over the knuckles of the right hand. I knew they had broken one of my fingers, because the skin spit apart and a splinter of bone stuck through. It hurt like all hell.

I tried to suck the blood away from where the splinter of bone stuck out of my finger, but they yanked my arm down and somebody hit me in the eye. Then somebody hit me in the other eye and I went blind. I couldn't see to protect myself.

I heard that first soft-voiced dick saying: "Wait a minute, fellows. I can't stand to see you treat him this way. Lay off a minute."

I knew he was working the old army on me, but I didn't care any more. I was glad for a couple of minutes' peace. I felt the soft-voiced guy helping me down into the chair, and he brought me a glass of water and held it to my mouth.

God, I wanted that water! But when I started to drink it, the bastard held it back and said: "Wait a minute, Pizzatello. Of course I want you to have this water. But don't you think you might return the favor by telling me all about how you killed Dr. Mason?"

"I didn't kill him."

"Sure you did, Pizzatello. But maybe you had good cause. Come on and open up. I'm your friend. I'll see that you don't get a hanging rap, if you'll spill to me."

I thought of something. "Sure I'll spill to you. I got something to tell you."

"That's better. Come on, let's have it."

"Give me the water first."

"No. You talk first, and then you can have all the water you want."

"Well, all right. Listen. You say there were two slugs taken out of Mason's cork leg that matched up with my roscoe. Is that right?"

"Yeah. That's right."

"But you didn't find the bullet that went through his brain and killed him?"

"No. We didn't look very hard. We didn't have to. The other two slugs are enough to pin it on you, Pizzatello."

"Well, look," I said. "I claim I shot Mason in the leg earlier this afternoon because he pulled a gun on me when he caught me with his wife. He was croaked later tonight. Well, I can prove I didn't fire the bullet that croaked him. I can prove it by my own gun."

"What do you mean, Pizzatello?"

"This afternoon, after I shot Mason in the leg, I went back to my apartment and reloaded my roscoe. When the cop took the gun away from me tonight in Mason's surgery, it was still loaded. It had a full clip. No bullets had been fired out of it. I grabbed the gun back from him when I biffed him, but you birds took it away from me again in my apartment when you put the pinch on me. The gat was still fully loaded. Now, if no slugs had been fired out of it tonight, that proves I didn't bump the doctor."

"Is that all you got to say, Pizzatello?"

"Yeah. Now give me that drink of water, for Christ's sake."

"I'll give you the water, you rat." And he threw the whole damned glassful right in my face.

Somebody said: "Okay, boys. Give him another taste of the stick. He seems to like it. Some guys are like that."

They grabbed me up out of the chair and made me stand on my feet, and then they started socking me again. I felt a fist smash into my mouth and two lower front teeth break off at the gum-line. I tried to spit them out, but my tongue and throat were all swollen and bloody and I couldn't. I choked and swallowed, and the teeth went down my throat. I said: "Oh, God—"

My lips were all puffed up like balloons. My eyes were closed, and I couldn't see to duck the blows that were battering at me. Somebody kicked me in the belly—away down. I curled over and grabbed myself and started to cry. I could feel the tears sliding down my cheeks and getting into my split lips, and the salt stung like hell, but I couldn't seem to stop crying.

Then somebody whaled me over the head with a billy, and a million lights blasted inside my brain, and I started to fold up because I couldn't take any more. I heard a far-away voice saying: "Look out, boys, he's caving. Catch him."

Then I didn't hear anything else.

Seven

WHEN I WOKE UP, I was back in my cell. I was lying on the lower cot, with a blanket over me, and it reminded me some of a Pullman lower berth—only it wasn't half as comfortable.

A little dim light was burning just outside the barred door of the cell, in the corridor, and I could see the glow by prying open my puffed eyelids with my fingers. But my eyes wouldn't stay open unless I held them.

I ached all over. There was a bandage around my head, and my broken finger was in splints, and my tongue kept sneaking to the places where three of my teeth had been batted out. The holes tasted raw and salty and bloody.

From the way I was bandaged, I knew I must have had medical attention after I passed out. Thinking about medical attention reminded me of Gertie Kohlar. What would become of her, now that I was in the clink? She needed money for an operation, but I wasn't in any position to get it for her, the way I was fixed.

I stirred around in my bunk and, every time I moved, it felt as if all the bones in my body had been busted. I called those third-degreeing plainclothes dicks all the names I could think of. I said: "I'll get even with the bastards some day!"

I didn't say it very loud, but my voice must have carried. All of a sudden, somebody whispered from above me: "Sh-h-h! Don't talk, or the screws will come in to see what's the matter, and they'll find me here in your cell, and then my goose will be cooked!"

At first I thought my ears were playing tricks on me. Then I realized the whisper must have come from the upper bunk, slung on chains over the one I was lying on. Somebody was up there over me.

I swung my legs out of bed and stood up so that my face was on a level with the upper bunk. I pried open one of my eyes and stared hard in the dim light. Then I said: "Well, for God's sake!"

It was a dame, and all she had on was a thin chemise. She was young-looking and she had a sort of pretty face, but her eyes looked hard. Her hair was bleached, and she didn't have any covers over her. She was just huddled on the bare matress, shivering. Her shape was nice, except that maybe her hips were a little too broad.

"Who the hell are you?" I asked her in a whisper.

"It don't matter who I am."

"How did you get in here?"

"The cops picked me up on a vag charge and brought me to jail tonight. They made me take a shower. When nobody was looking, I slipped out of the shower and ran down the corridor. I thought maybe I could make a getaway. But I heard somebody coming, and I saw a cell door open, so I ducked in. I climbed up here on the top bunk and hid myself, and then they brought you in on a stretcher and dumped you on the lower bunk. They locked the door and went away and didn't see me. So here I am."

I noticed goose-pimples all over her bare arms and legs. "You're cold, kiddo."

"Y-yes. I'm freezing."

"Come on down to my bunk and crawl under the blanket."

"You—you d-don't mind?"

"Sure not. Come on down."

I helped her climb down, and I covered her with my blanket. Then I sat alongside her on the edge of the bunk. She snuggled up to me and tried to warm herself by getting as close to me as she could.

I put my arm around her and touched her breast, soft and sort of squidgy. She didn't seem to mind it very much when I touched her there.

After a while, she put her mouth up close to my ear and whispered; "Jeeze, but they certainly musta pounded you to a pulp, didn't they, big boy?"

"Yeah. They worked me over. They gave me the third degree and busted a finger for me."

"What for?"

"Trying to make me confess to a phoney murder rap."

"What's your name, honey?"

"Duke Pizzatello."

"Are you really a murderer?"

"No."

"They framed you?"

"Yeah. They framed me."

"They framed me, too—on a vagrancy charge. I'm no tramp. This is the first time I ever been in jail in my life."

I said: "If they catch you here in my cell, you'll stay in jail a hell of a long time, I'm thinking."

She drew a long breath and pressed as close to me as she could get. "Ain't there some way I might lam out of here?"

"I wish I thought so. I'd go with you," I said.

She said: "You figure a way for us to get out, and I'll be—plenty nice to you." She pressed my hand up against her breast.

I said: "Lay off, sister. I don't feel like playing. Those coppers socked hell out of me. They kicked me in the groin. Besides, I can't figure any way out of here. If I could, I'd be gone long ago."

She sighed and said: "I sorta wish you felt better, honey. You thrill me, just being close to me this way."

"You must thrill awful easy, then."

"No. But—but it's what you told me."

"What I told you?"

"Yes. About you being here on a murder rap. I've always wondered what it would be like to be made love to by a killer."

"Don't be screwy, sister. I told you the murder rap was a phoney. I'm no murderer. I was framed."

"Oh, stop being coy. It's okay to tell me everything. You can trust me." She shrugged down the shoulder-straps of her chemise and said: "Snuggle down here and get the load off your chest. Tell me how you came to croak Dr. Mason."

I sat up and said: "You damned bitch, I never mentioned Mason's name!" Then I grabbed her wrists with my one good hand and said: "Goddam you, you're a police stoolie. The cops planted you here in my cell to get around me and make me spill my guts!"

"No!"

I twisted her arms. "Come on, admit it, you slut!"

"No! No!"

I twisted some more. "Admit it, or else I'll bat your teeth down your throat!"

"Stop it! You're hurting me!"

"I ought to kill you. You lied about being pinched and escaping here to my cell. It was all a cock-and-bull story, wasn't it?"

She started to scream.

I said: "When the dicks couldn't pry anything out of me with their fists, they planted you in here with me. They figured maybe I'd fall for you and make love to you and then go soft all over and spill my innards, huh?"

"I—yes—"

"Damn you!" I said. By now, she was screaming at the top of her lungs and yelling like all hell. My cell door clanged open, and two screws jumped in and tackled me and threw me down.

The dame stood on her feet and glared at me. "The louse wouldn't tell me a thing!" she said to the two screws. She turned and bounced out of my cell.

The two keepers tossed me back in my bunk and went out. They locked the cell door and turned out the light in the corridor.

Eight

AFTER A WHILE I fell asleep. Once, a little before dawn, I sort of half woke up, and it seemed somebody was in my cell, staring down at me. But before I could tell whether it was real or just a dream, I fell all the way asleep again, and the next time I woke up it was daylight.

The swelling around my left eye had gone down a little, and I could see through a thin slit between the upper and lower lids. Grey light was probing in through my barred windows, and I heard a lot of footsteps in the corridor outside.

I looked around and saw some people standing at the door of my cell. There were three screws, a well-tailored guy, and—Dixie Parker!

"Hello, Wop," she said.

She was dressed in a sport skirt and a tight-clinging blue sweater that outlined her breast-works, and she looked a little tired around the eyes. One of the screws unlocked my cell door and Dixie came in, rolling her hips as usual.

She said: "They must have handed you a sweet trimming last night, Duke."

"Yeah. I got a busted finger."

"The dirty tramps! Well, it's all right. You're going out of here with me now."

"Out of here? What do you mean, babe?"

"I got you released on bail-bond. Steve and Joe Kohlar signed the bond." Then Dixie pointed to the well-tailored guy. "This is District Attorney Terhune. He okayed your release."

The guy said: "Yes, Mr. Pizzatello. And I hope you will overlook the overzealousness of the police last night." He sounded like a man making a political speech. He went on: "They exceeded their authority when they struck you. Of course, you understand that you are merely out on bond, and you will be required to present yourself at the coroner's inquest. Later on, you may be asked to face a grand jury."

"Sure," I said.

But I couldn't get it through my skull that I was being turned loose. It didn't make sense. And why should the D.A. admit that the cops had put me through the ringer? That didn't add up right, either. I know police methods. They make a pinch, and they beat hell out of a guy, and then, if the guy makes a beef through his lawyer, they claim they never hit him at all, but that he was all bunged up when they arrested him.

Dixie took me out to her little roadster and we drove off. I said: "How the hell did you work it, babe?"

"It was easy. I had the cops by the short hair."

"Nobody ever gets the cops by the short hair," I said.

"Well, I did. You remember, I made you take off your clothes last night, and then I took your picture holding the front page of last night's newspaper?"

"Yeah. Sure I remember."

"Well, I had a reason for that. I knew you were about to be nabbed, and I knew what the dicks would do to you. So I took that picture, and the newspaper date-line proved the photo had been made last night, just before your arrest. At the time of the picture, you didn't have a single bruise on you. Get it?"

"I'm beginning to get it."

"You see," Dixie explained, "I persuaded the district attorney to come to your cell with me at dawn this morning. After he saw how you were all battered up, I showed

him the picture I had taken of you just before you were
arrested. The photo proved you were in good shape before
you were taken to jail. It proved the cops must have slammed you around after your arrest."

I said: "Smart girl! So it was you and the D.A. who
were in my cell around dawn, huh? I thought there was
somebody looking at me, but it seemed almost like a
dream. Well, anyhow, after the D.A. saw the evidence,
what happened?"

Dixie said: "I made a deal with him. I agreed you
wouldn't make any squawk about being beaten up if he
gave you a release on bond. He said all right, and I got
the Kohlar boys to sign the bond, and here you are."

She parked her roadster, and I saw that we were outside
the office building where we both worked for the Kohlars.
We went upstairs, and Joe Kohlar was in the outer office.
He looked at me without smiling, and his washed-out blue
eyes made me shiver a little. "So you got loose, did you?"
he said.

"Yeah, Joe, thanks to you and Steve for going my bail."

"Don't thank me. Thank Steve. He's the one that talked
me into signing your bond with him." Joe's voice was like
a chunk of ice, cold and brittle.

Just then Steve Kohlar's private door opened and Steve
motioned for me to come in. After the door was closed, he
grinned at Dixie and me and said: "Don't pay any attention
to Joe this morning. He's got a grouch. Wife trouble."

I felt a funny tightness in my throat. "You mean Joe
and Gertie are scrapping?"

Steve nodded. "Yeah. Remember last night, after you
discovered those corpses in Mason's surgery, Duke? You
came out to our house to tell me about the jam you were
in. Joe wasn't home at the time, so I went into Gertie's
room and gave her a message for him before I went out
with you."

I said: "Sure. I remember."

"Well, Joe didn't come home all night. He was on a

binge. When he showed up at the house this morning,
Gertie was gone. I guess she got sore at him for staying
out all night. Anyhow, she left him a note telling him she
was going to Chicago to visit her sister. Now he's grouchy
as hell."

I tried to keep the jitters out of my face. So Gertie had
pulled up stakes! And she had used the excuse she told
me she was going to use—a visit to her sister in Chi. I
wondered where she had got hold of the money to pay her
way. Of course I knew she wasn't really headed for
Chicago, but to a hospital in some nearby town instead.
I wondered if she would get in touch with me.

But I kept my thoughts to myself. I covered up by saying: "It was damned decent of you and Joe to sign my
bond, Steve."

He waved his hand. "Forget it. Now that you're out,
we've got to start working to find out who croaked Mason
and his broad."

I said: "We won't have to look very far. Mrs. Mason is
the one. She came down to the jail last night and pretended
she didn't know me. She threw me to the wolves. You and
I both figured out, if she did that instead of fronting for
me, it would mean she was probably the guilty one. She's
trying to frame me to keep her own skirts clear, the bitch."

Steve looked thoughtful. "Yeah, it looks that way. She
acted plenty queer last night when I saw her and tried to
talk her into giving you an alibi. She even tried to deny
she'd ever been in this office. I told her she couldn't get
away with that, because it would be her lone word against
all of ours. Dixie saw her in here, and I talked with her,
and you went out with her. That makes three against one.
But she said she'd deny it, anyhow, and the cops would
believe her—because they'd think Dixie and I were just
trying to get you out of your jam."

I said: "Damn her soul!"

Then Steve settled back in his chair. "However, Duke,
we can't be too sure Nelia Mason is the killer. There's a
new angle that's come up in the case."

"A new angle?"

"Yes. You remember Mason had a partner in his medical bungalow—a Dr. Willoughby Sebring?"

"I remember. I never saw the guy, though."

"Well, it's come out that this Dr. Sebring has been having trouble with Mason lately. They were sort of sore at each other. And now Sebring has taken it on the lam. He's disappeared, and nobody seems to know where he went."

"The hell you preach!" I said. "What did he and Mason fight about; does anybody know?"

"Yes. From what I've gathered, they scrapped over the nurse who worked for them as office-girl and receptionist. Her name was Myra Holly— And listen, Duke: this Holly girl has also disappeared!"

"Jesus!"

"Yeah. Right now the bulls are working on the theory that maybe the carved-up female corpse is Myra Holly. Of course she was so damned sliced up that identification is impossible, but—"

I said: "Christ! Then maybe Sebring and Mason were both nuts over this nurse, and she picked Mason, and that made Sebring jealous, huh? So maybe Sebring bumped Mason and the nurse and carved her up and then beat it?"

Steve shrugged. "It's a theory, at least."

"Then what do you think I should ought to do, boss?" I said.

"Strikes me you'd better start looking for Dr. Sebring. Put the finger on him, and maybe he'll cough up some information."

"Sebring!" I said. "Him being a doctor and surgeon might account for the way the dead dame's carcass was all cut up with a scalpel, huh?"

"Perhaps."

"Then I got to start looking for him!" I said.

Dixie Parker spoke up. "I'll drive you wherever you want to go, Wop."

"Thanks, babe."

Dixie and I went downstairs and got in her roadster. I said: "Take me to my apartment, babe. I want to catch a shave and change my clothes and patch up my mug a little."

"Okay, Duke."

She drove me to my place, and we went upstairs. When I unlocked my door, there was a letter in the slot. I picked it up.

It was from Gertie Kohlar, special delivery. It had been mailed just that same morning.

Nine

I TURNED AROUND To Dixie. "Excuse me a minute, babe, while I read my fan mail."

"Sure, Duke. Go ahead." Dixie lit a cigarette and took off her hat and sat down on the sofa.

I ripped open the envelope and read Gertie Kohlar's letter. Gertie's handwriting was kind of punk, but I made out all right:

"Dear Duke—

I am pulling out this morning and leaving a note for Joe telling him I am going to Chi to visit my sis. But I am really taking a bus for up north, and I will go to a certain doctor in Fresno who does those kind of operations. Joe don't suspect nothing, so you needn't worry. When I get located in Fresno, I will drop you a line and you can send me the money we talked about last night. I am taking forty dollars I had saved up, but that won't be near enough to pay everything, so be ready to send me some dough as soon as I let you know my address in Fresno, because you know the doctor will want cash in advance.

Lovingly,
Gertie."

I read the letter again, and then I began to sweat, because it's dangerous to write that sort of stuff on paper. And besides, here Gertie was expecting me to send her some money, and how the hell could I send her any dough in my present fix?

I knew I wouldn't have time to go out and earn any important jack for a while, because my hands would be plenty full trying to solve the Mason murder mystery. Unless I broke the case pretty quick, I would have to go before the grand jury, and I would maybe be indicted and thrown back in the jug, and then I would be tied up good and proper.

And yet I had to get some money for Gertie, because, if I didn't, she might get sore and do something to get even with me. She might even spill her guts to Joe, and, if that happened, he would be mad as hell and God knows what he might do.

About the only place I could think of where I might get some shekels was Nelia Mason's. Maybe, if I went to see her, I could scare a couple hundred dollars out of her and, at the same time, kill two birds with one stone by making her admit she was with me the night her old man got croaked, thus giving me an alibi.

All this flashed through my brain faster than it takes to tell, and meanwhile I was tearing up Gertie's letter into little pieces. I took the pieces and lit a match and set fire to them. I threw them in the tin wastebasket and watched them burn to ashes. Then I felt better.

Dixie Parker looked at me. "Destroying a love letter from your sweetie, Wop?"

"Hell, no. I haven't got any sweetie. That was a business letter, babe."

"The deuce it was. It was from a dame. It looked like a woman's handwriting on the envelope."

"Okay, then. It was from a dame. So what?"

"Oh, nothing."

"Why should you care how many letters I get from dames?"

Dixie looked at me harder and patted back her yellow hair. When she put her arms over her head that way, her breasts made round mounds under her blue sweater. All of a sudden two tears started rolling down her cheeks and she began to cry. "Damn you, Duke, you're the dumbest guy I ever knew!"

"Dumb? Me?"

"Yes. Why do you suppose I went through all I did to get you out of jail on bond?"

"Damned if I know, Dixie. I been wondering about that myself. Why did you?"

"Oh, you thick-skulled Italian ape! I did it because I— because—I—" She jumped up and ran across to me, and put her arms around me and her head on my shoulder and sobbed to beat hell.

I said: "What the devil, babe—?"

"Shut up! Shut up and let me cry my darned eyes out! It doesn't mean anything to you, anyhow. You don't even know I exist! You don't even realize I'm a woman. Every day down at the office, you grin and make passes at me when you get a chance, and it doesn't mean any more to you than p-patting a d-dog. I guess—"

"Jesus, babe, I didn't think—"

"—I guess it never struck you I might be human—might want you to hold me in your arms and k-kiss me once in a while—"

"For God's sake, Dixie, I didn't know you felt that way about me." I was holding her and patting her, and her breasts were against my chest, and all of a sudden I realized what she wanted. I kissed her on the mouth, and she clung to me and sort of moaned a little.

So then I pulled her over to the couch, and she snuggled down on the cushions and held her arms out to me, and then neither of us said anything more, but just lost ourselves.

After a while she sighed and looked at me. "Duke."

"Yeah, babe?"

"Tell me what really happened yesterday afternoon when you put those bullets in Dr. Mason's cork leg."

"Nothing happened, Dixie. Not what you think, anyhow. I didn't pull any rough stuff with Mrs. Mason. She took off her negligee to show me the bruises where her husband beat her, and then he walked in—just as she threw herself in my arms for no damned reason. He went for his rod, and I let him have a couple, and then I lammed."

"She threw herself in your arms just as he walked in?"

"Yeah. The way I doped it out, she wanted him croaked. She was trying to frame me into bumping him."

Dixie's eyes narrowed. "You doped it out that she tried to frame you into murdering her husband. And yet you went right back to her again last night and let her put you on the spot!"

I said: "Well, I had to. I didn't want to go back to her, after the way you invited me to stay with you in your apartment. But I couldn't help myself. Mrs. Mason was going to pay me some important dough to get a picture of the doctor and his broad for divorce evidence. I needed that dough, babe. I needed it bad. That's why I went back to her and got tricked into going into that damned surgery."

"You needed money, Wop?"

"Yeah. I'll say."

"What for?"

I decided I might as well spill everything, now that Dixie and I were so close. So I said: "I needed it to give to Gertie Kohlar."

"Gertie Kohlar? Joe's wife?"

"Yeah. Gertie's in trouble. She blames it on me. I never was out with her, only once. I met her on a party when we were both fried, and we sort of forgot ourselves. I was plenty sorry afterward, but that didn't help any. Yesterday Gertie came to me and told me the fix she was in. She couldn't blame it on Joe because—well, he got wounded in France during the war."

"I'll bet that letter you just tore up was from Gertie, wasn't it?"

"Yeah. She's gone to a doctor in Fresno, and I got to send her some cash pretty quick."

"And where do you figure to get some cash, Duke?"

"Well, I thought of going to see Nelia Mason. Maybe I can wangle a couple of hundred fish out of her. And, at the same time, maybe I can force her to admit she was with me last night, and give me an alibi to prove I didn't croak her husband."

"Duke—don't go see that woman. Please. For my sake. She's dangerous. I know. I can feel it. If you play around with her or even see her, she'll put your neck in a noose!"

I didn't feel like arguing. So, to save time, I said: "Okay, babe. If you feel that strongly about it, I'll take your advice. I'll steer clear of her."

Dixie got up and smoothed down her blue sweater and patted her yellow hair. "What are you going to do the rest of the day?"

"I'll go see a dentist and try to have a couple temporary teeth put in the front of my mouth, where mine got knocked out last night."

"After that, what?"

"Well, I'll smell around and see if I can pick up some trace of that Dr. Willoughby Sebring. Maybe I can find him and get some information out of him."

"That's a good angle, Duke. Do you want me to drive you to the dentist's first?"

"No, thanks, babe. My own jaloppy's in the garage downstairs. I'll use it. Thanks all the same."

"Can you drive all right with that broken finger?"

"Oh, sure. The splints don't get in my way much."

"Well, okay, then. I'll be going back to the office. Kiss me, Duke."

I kissed her.

At the front door, she said: "Promise me you won't go near Mrs. Mason?"

"Yeah. I promise, babe."

But I had my fingers crossed when I said it.

Ten

I TOOK A SHOWER and changed into fresh underwear and sox and shirt and a freshly pressed suit. I went to a bureau drawer and got out a spare automatic I kept there and slipped it into my coat pocket. Then I went downstairs and oozed into my coupé and drove out to Nelia Mason's house.

A colored maid opened the door. "Yes, suh?"

"I want to see Mrs. Mason."

"Sorry, suh, Mrs. Mason ain't at home to reporters or nobody." She looked suspiciously at my black eyes.

"I'm not a reporter. You go tell Mrs. Mason a man from the insurance company wants to see her about a policy her late husband carried."

"Yes, suh. I'll tell her. You wait right here." And she closed the door in my face.

I turned my back, in case Nelia Mason might look through the glass in the door and spot me and see who I was. Pretty soon the door opened again and the maid said: "Mrs. Mason's in bed, suh, with a sick headache, but she said she'd see you a minute. You come along with me."

I said: "Never mind taking me up to her room. Just tell me which door it is upstairs, and I'll go on up. I got personal things to discuss with Mrs. Mason. You understand."

"Yes, suh. It's the first front room on the second floor."

I went upstairs and forward along the hall until I came to a partly open door. I dragged out my roscoe and held it in my left hand, because of the splints on that busted finger of my right.

Inside the room, somebody said: "Come in, insurance man."

Holding the rod in front of me, I shoved the door open with my foot and walked into the bedroom. I said: "Don't scream, because, if you do, I'll put a slug through your teeth."

Mrs. Mason was lying on the bed, wearing a black negligee with nothing much underneath it, and, when she saw me, she turned a sort of greenish color. She said: "You! Pizzatello!"

"Yeah, me." I kicked the door shut and went over to the bed and perched on the edge of it. I held my roscoe close to Nelia Mason's left breast, shoving it pretty deep into the softness of her flesh to let her know I wasn't fooling.

"Wh—what do you want?" she whispered.

I grinned at her. It was probably an ugly grin, because of those two teeth missing at the front of my mouth. "I want a couple of things," I said. "In the first place, I want some dough."

"For murdering my husband?"

"You know goddam well I didn't bump him. No, I want money to pay me for the jam you got me in."

"I don't know what you're talking about. How did I get you in a jam?"

"You got a nerve to ask me that, after you pretended you didn't know me last night downtown at the jail!" I said.

"I—I didn't want to get mixed up in it at all."

I said: "Sure not—because you croaked your husband yourself! I'm hep to you. You wanted your old man knocked off. So you came to the Kohlar detective agency and pretended you wanted a private dick to get divorce evidence. Then you framed things so the doctor would walk in and catch you and me together. You figured he'd go for his rod, and you hoped I'd beat him to the draw. You thought I'd kill him in self-defense. But, instead, I only hit his cork leg and then lammed. So, later last night, you caught him in his surgery with a dame—and you shot him and carved the dame. Then, just by luck, you got word from Steve Kohlar that I was willing to go through with the divorce evidence job you'd asked me to handle for you. You suddenly saw a way to frame me for the murders you had done yourself. So you pretended the doctor was still alive, and you hoaxed me into walking into his surgery and finding the two bodies. Then you left me in the lurch."

She said: "That's not so, Mr. Pizzatello! I—I drove away in your car because I was suddenly scared. I didn't know my husband was already dead. I thought you might get into another gun-fight with him, and I got frightened and drove away so I wouldn't hear the sound of the shots. So help me God, that's the truth."

"You lie in your teeth. You killed him and tried to frame me for it!"

"No—no—no!"

I said: "Now see here, sweetheart. There's no use arguing about this thing. Personally, I think you're guilty as hell. But, on the other hand, maybe you're innocent. I don't give a damn, either way, as long as you get me out of the mess and clear my skirts."

"How can I clear your skirts?"

"By signing a statement that you and I went to your husband's medical bungalow last night to get divorce evidence against him, and that I wasn't in there long enough to do any killing or carving."

"I won't sign any such paper. It would drag me into the case. It might make the police suspect me."

"No, it wouldn't. I'm offering you a chance to get clear—along with me. You pay me three hundred fish and sign that statement and we'll both stick to it. I'll be your alibi and you'll be mine. We'll both go free. The cops won't be able to pin anything on either of us." I looked at her. "You'll also have to admit that I was here in the house with you yesterday afternoon, and that the doctor caught us and I had to shoot him in self-defense. That will clear me about the two slugs from my gun that were found in his cork leg when he was dead."

"Sign away my reputation? I won't!"

I said: "The hell you won't. You'll do like I say, or I'll make you wish you had never been born."

"What do you mean?"

"I'll give you a sample of what I mean." I reached forward and grabbed her the best I could with my damaged right hand. I dropped my roscoe on the bed and doubled my left fist and started to biff her on the shoulders. I ripped her negligee open in front, and I guess I sort of went a little crazy for a minute.

But before I could hit her even once, she closed her eyes and folded over and went limp. I realized she must have fainted from fright, and I grabbed her shoulders and shook her so that her head bobbed around and her bare breasts jiggled up and down. I said: "Damn you, wake up and take your medicine!"

But she didn't open her eyes, and her breath was wheezing in her throat. Then, all of a sudden, a voice behind me said: "Put up your hands, Wop!"

Eleven

I GOT STIFF all over, and a cold chill went down my spine, and my mouth tingled inside as if I had put my tongue on an electric battery. I got slowly to my feet and put my arms in the air and looked around, and there was Dixie Parker, standing in the doorway of the bedroom with a roscoe leveled at my guts.

Her eyes were blazing and her lips were curled and she looked sore as hell. "You want another murder rap hanging over your head, you fool?"

I said: "Don't be nutty. I wasn't trying to bump her. I was just trying to make her come across with something I wanted."

"Yes, and now you've let yourself in for plenty more grief. Come on. We're getting out of here."

"Okay, babe. Put away the rod. I'll go with you."

"Like hell I'll put away the rod. You'd probably take a poke at me and bat me into the middle of next Tuesday!"

"I wouldn't do a thing like that to you, babe. You know I wouldn't."

"I don't trust you any further than I can throw a bull by the tail. I had a hunch you'd come here and maybe do something like this. That's why I followed you here."

"You followed me?"

"Yes, in a taxi. I figured you were probably lying when you told me you were going to the dentist. I slipped the colored maid downstairs two bucks to let me sneak up here, and it's a lucky thing I did. This is what I get for trusting you and getting you out of jail. Come on, get going."

"Where to?"

"I ought to turn you back into custody. Maybe I will. You'd be safer in a cell, you lame-brain. Let's go before Mrs. Mason comes to and starts yelling her head off."

She prodded me with her gun, and there wasn't anything I could do except obey orders. We went out of the bedroom and down the stairs, and we didn't see the maid hanging around anywhere. We went out to my coupe and got in, and I drove, while Dixie kept her gat jammed against my ribs.

After a while, I said: "Where shall I drive to?"

"My apartment."

"It strikes me you're acting mighty goddam funny about this thing, babe."

"Am I?"

"Yeah. I thought you were a friend of mine."

"I thought so, too. Now I'm not so sure."

"Why aren't you so sure?"

"Because you promised me you'd stay away from Mrs. Mason, and you broke your promise."

"Why should you think so damned much of the Mason bimbo?"

"I don't care anything about her."

"Then why should you worry if I socked her a little?"

"It's you I'm worried about, not Mrs. Mason. Besides, why should you sock her?"

"I was trying to get something out of her."

"What were you trying to get, a ticket to the noose?"

"Don't be funny. I was trying to get her to sign a statement that she was with me last night, and that I wasn't in her husband's surgery long enough to bump him and his broad."

"You idiot, you might know she wouldn't sign anything like that."

"Yeah. I found it out. That's why I was going to biff her. She tried to tell me she ran out on me last night because she was scared I'd get into another gun-fight with Mason. That's a goddam lie. She knew I couldn't get into another gun-fight with him, because she knew he was dead. She knew it because she had bumped him herself, the way I figure."

By that time we were in front of Dixie's apartment. I parked; then we went upstairs to her flat. Dixie closed the door and stared at me and said: "Duke, did it ever strike you that maybe Mrs. Mason isn't lying? That maybe she's telling the truth, and didn't know her husband was dead when she sent you into his surgery?"

"No. It never struck me. Why should I believe that? We know Mrs. Mason wanted the doctor croaked, because she tried to trick me into doing it for her yesterday afternoon. The way I got it doped out, when I didn't cut the mustard, she decided to kill him herself. She caught him and his sweetie in the surgery later last night, and plugged him through the skull and cut the broad's throat and sliced her up. Then she left the two corpses in the surgery and went home. A little later, I got in touch with her through Steve Kohlar and told her I was willing to go through with the deal to get divorce evidence for her, because I needed dough. She saw a way to frame the killings on me, so she tricked me into going down to Mason's surgery with my camera. Then she drove off and left me to take the rap. And now she refuses to give me an alibi, even though she knows I wasn't in that bungalow long enough to shoot Mason or slice up his girl friend."

Dixie said: "Wait a minute, Wop. Right there is where you've put your finger on something."

"What do you mean?"

"I mean the corpse of that dead woman."

"What about it?"

"Plenty. Let me ask you a question. If your theory is true and Mrs. Mason is the murderer, why should she cut up her husband's sweetie's carcass?"

"I don't know. Probably because the Mason woman is a savage bitch and would do something like that for revenge on the dame who was chasing around with her husband."

"No, Duke. The way that dead woman was carved up doesn't indicate plain blind fury on the part of the killer."

"What does it indicate, then?"

"To me, it indicates that the murderer deliberately set out to destroy every chance of identifying the dead woman."

"Why should Mrs. Mason not want the dame to be identified?"

"That's just it. She'd have no motive for such a thing. Therefore I don't think she's guilty. If Mrs. Mason had killed her husband and his mistress, she wouldn't have gone to all the trouble to destroy the woman's identity. She'd have just shot them both and let it go at that."

"So what?"

"So, on that basis, I think we can eliminate Mrs. Mason as a suspect."

"And where the hell does that leave us?"

Dixie said: "It leaves us to think about Dr. Willoughby Sebring, who has disappeared. The doctor who was Mason's medical partner. Remember, Sebring and Mason had quarreled over their nurse, Myra Holly—who also is missing."

"So you're coming around to Steve Kohlar's theory, huh?" I said. "You think maybe Dr. Sebring killed Mason and the nurse? You think the carved-up dame was Myra Holly?"

"Not necessarily. Put it this way. Suppose Dr. Sebring murdered Dr. Mason. But, meanwhile, suppose Mason had secretly had a woman in that bungalow with him. Suppose she accidentally witnessed the murder. Then suppose Sebring found her and realized she had seen the whole thing. Sebring would then have to kill the woman, too—to keep her mouth shut. Then perhaps he got scared and ran away, which accounts for his disappearance."

Dixie rattled all that stuff off pretty fast, but I thought I caught a tone to her voice that didn't sound convincing. It was like she was talking just to hear herself talk.

I wondered why she should be trying to string me. She was acting like she wanted to steer me away from being suspicious of Nelia Mason. That struck me as damned funny. Why should Dixie front for the Mason woman?

I decided to see just how far she'd go. So I pretended to be interested in her theory. I said: "Okay, babe. Supposing all this stuff you're saying is true. Then why should Dr. Sebring carve up the dame after croaking her? And what became of the nurse, Myra Holly?"

"Maybe Myra Holly took a run-out powder with Sebring when he lammed. Maybe she helped him do the killing. Maybe she was with him on the whole thing."

Before I could come back at that one, her phone rang. Dixie got up and picked up the receiver and said: "Hello?"

She listened a minute, then looked across at me and got a funny expression in her eyes. She lowered her voice and mumbled something into the phone that I couldn't catch.

Then she hung up and came toward me. "My beauty parlor was calling about an apointment I've got for this afternoon."

She was lying. I could tell it. "Yeah?"

"Yes. So I guess you'll have to beat it, Duke. I think you'd better get going and see if you can pick up any trace of Dr. Willoughby Sebring."

"You mean you want me to scram out of here?"

"Well, there's no use your staying around here any longer, wasting time. But you've got to promise you won't go out to Mrs. Mason's house again."

"Okay, babe. And I'll keep my word this time."

She smiled at me. "I believe you, Duke. Let's have a drink on it."

"Sure, kiddo."

She went into her kitchenette and came back with two snorts of rye. She handed me one and I tossed it down. The minute it went down my gullet, I knew it was doped. It sort of burned my throat and my belly, and it made me feel sick. I threw the glass on the floor and made a jump at Dixie and said: "What the hell have you pulled on me?"

Her face got pale, and she snatched her roscoe from the table where she had laid it when we first came in. She leveled the gat at me and said: "Sit down, Wop."

I sat down. I began to feel woozy, and I knew I had been double-crossed plenty, but I couldn't understand why. My eyelids began to get heavy all of a sudden, and the room started going around in circles, and the floor was rocking up and down.

I knew Dixie had fed me a Mickey Finn, and I knew she had done it on account of that phone call she had just got. But I couldn't figure it out. In a minute I couldn't figure anything out. I went to sleep, with the floor rocking up and down under my feet.

Twelve

WHEN I WOKE UP, I was lying on my back, and things were still rocking up and down under me, but somehow in a different way. I opened my eyes and tried to see, but it was too dark to tell anything about where I was.

I sat up and bumped my head against something. I felt around and found I was in a bunk or berth, and that there was another bunk over me. That was what I had bumped my head on.

So then I figured I was back in a jail cell. Dixie Parker had doped me and then turned me back over to the cops. I began to curse her for double-crossing me that way, but, all the time I was cursing her, I was puzzled because I didn't understand why she should turn against me so completely. And what was that mysterious phone call Dixie had got, just before she slipped me the Mickey Finn?

The more I tried to think, the buzzier my head got. I was feeling sick and, as I sat there in the darkness, it seemed as if the bunk was going up and down under me all the time. Up and down, up and down, like a boat in a ground-swell.

I swung my feet over the side of the bunk and felt the floor with them, and the floor kept moving like I was drunk. Then, all of a sudden, I heard a voice in the bunk above mine. It startled hell out of me.

"Oh, my God. I've got to get out of here. Oh, my God. I've got to get some fresh air. Oh, my *God!* my head hurts!"

For a minute I thought it was another dirty police trick. I thought the dicks had planted another stoolie in my cell with me, and I went crazy mad. I scratched a match that I found in my pocket and held it up over the upper bunk. I took a squint at the guy lying there.

He was a little shrimp, about forty-five, and he had a big blue bruise over his left temple, and his eyes were wide and staring and sort of vacant-looking. His hair was grey at the edges and all tousled, and he needed a shave and looked pale as a ghost.

I said: "You goddam stool-pigeon!" and grabbed him and yanked him down out of his bunk. He fell on the floor and couldn't stand up, so I lifted him to his feet and steadied him. I said: "So you think you can do some play-acting and gain my confidence and make me talk, huh?"

He started to whimper and moan. "Don't hit me, Mister. Oh, my God, I've got to get out of here. I've got to have fresh air. Oh, my *God,* my head hurts!"

"It'll hurt you a hell of a lot worse when I get through with you, you goddam lousy rat of a stoolie!" I shook him, and he went to his knees, and put his arms around my legs and held on to me, and his whole thin little body trembled like he had the ague.

I began to feel ashamed of myself for getting rough with him, he looked so little and skinny and puny. Of course my match had gone out long ago, but, by this time, my eyes were a little accustomed to the darkness, and I could just manage to see the little fellow's outlines as he knelt at my feet and moaned.

I fumbled in my pocket and found another match. I struck it and lifted the little guy to his pins and looked at that nasty blue bruise on his left temple. It was swollen like a duck egg, and the skin was broken. "Who the hell are you?" I asked him.

"Who am I? I—I don't know, Mister. I don't know. Oh, my God, I've got to get out of here and get some fresh air! Oh, my *God,* my head hurts!"

"How did you get that knot on your dome?"

"How did I get it?" His hand went to his forehead and he felt that swollen lump of a bruise. "I don't know how I got it, Mister. But, oh, *God,* it hurts!"

"Listen. Just who the hell are you, anyhow?" I asked him again.

"I don't know who I am. I can't seem to remember. I can't remember my name or anything. But my head hurts. Take me out of here and let me get some fresh air, Mister. Please. Where am I?"

I started to laugh at him and then, for some reason, I didn't. I lit a third match and took another gander at him, and his eyes were empty and pleading, like a dog's. Either he was leveling with me, or he was the best goddam actor I ever saw.

"You're in jail, buddy," I told him. "You're in a cell in the jail-house."

"Jail? How did I get here? Listen, Mister. You've got to get me out. I must have fresh air. I'm smothering, and my head hurts."

I said: "You'll have a hell of a time getting out of here, buddy. But maybe I can get a screw to come here and look you over and maybe get the prison doctor for you." I steadied him and started away from the bunk with him, feeling my way in the darkness for the door of the cell.

The little guy kept moaning as I helped him along, and we wandered along three walls of the cell without finding any door. All I found was a lot of other bunks on the three walls. That struck me as damned funny, because I had never seen a jail cell with so many bunks before.

I didn't find a door, but, all of a sudden, I stumbled on some steps. And, somehow, the steps and the floor seemed to be moving up and down under me. And when I looked up the steps, I saw an opening—a sort of slanted trapdoor that was wide open. Beyond the trapdoor, I could see the dark sky and the stars twinkling and shining.

I helped the little guy up the steps and, when we got to the top, I looked around me and said: "Jesus, this is no jail. We're on a boat!"

Thirteen

IT WAS TRUE. We were on the deck of a little schooner of some sort. That was why things kept going up and down under my feet. It was the lazy swell of the waves making the boat rock.

The little fellow said: "Oh, my God! Fresh air!" He ran to the rail and leaned over and looked at the black water and drew in big, gasping breaths, filling his lungs. He was still wobbly on his feet, and he coughed a little.

For a minute, I stood still, trying to pull myself together. It was a hell of a shock, finding myself out on the ocean, when I had thought I was in the jug.

I didn't know a damned thing about how I had got where I was. But I realized Dixie must have done it. She had doped me and shanghaied me.

It suddenly struck me that I was worse off than if she had taken me back to jail. Because now I didn't know where I was, or how far away I was from home. And, meanwhile, the cops might be looking all over hell for me, thinking I had jumped my bond. And when a guy jumps his bond, it's almost a confession of guilt.

Just about then I saw a big, beefy guy walking along the deck. He came to the little fellow at the rail. "What the hell you doin' on deck, bozo? You better go below an' cork off some more, because your watch is an hour from now, when we make port."

"Mister, I had to come up here and get some fresh air. Oh, God, my head hurts. How did I get on this boat?"

"How did you get on this boat?" The beefy man laughed and spat over the rail. "You poor punk, you was loafin' around the docks in San Pedro this afternoon, an' you come aboard an' asked for grub. I offered you a job, an' you signed on for the voyage."

"I don't remember that, Mister. I don't remember anything. But I don't want to be on this boat. I want to get off. I've got something to do. I don't remember what it is, but I've got something to do, and it's important. Let me off the boat, please, Mister."

"Let you off—hell! Listen, mug. We're comin' into San Diego harbor right away, an' if you try to jump ship, I'll keelhaul you."

"Keelhaul me? I don't understand. What does that mean? And why can't I get off the boat?"

"You'll find out damn quick if you try an' start anything, bozo. Now go below till you're called on watch." The beefy guy put his hands on the little fellow's shoulders and shoved him.

The little man went to his knees, he was so weak. In the light of a lamp from the deck-house, I saw that the beefy bird was wearing a cap that said: "MATE." He had a tough face and a square jaw. He drew back his brogan and started to kick the little fellow.

That got me sore. I jumped forward out of the shadows. "Don't touch that guy. He's sick, can't you see? You leave him alone!"

The mate looked around and saw me for the first time. He started to grin. "Oh! The mug which that dame brought aboard, huh? So you got over your souse, did you?"

I said: "I don't know how I got aboard or who brought me, but I'm telling you to lay off the little guy. He's sick."

"I'll make him sicker, the shrimp. An' you might as well learn right now you're only a deck-hand this voyage, an' I'm first officer, an' I won't take no lip off of you." The mate lashed out with his foot and kicked the little man.

The little guy groaned and went flat on the deck on his face. He was sick to his stomach and vomited a little, and laid there with his face in the vomit. I said: "You great big goddam son of a bitch!" and jumped at the mate, swinging my mitts.

I couldn't do much with my right hand on account of the splint on my broken finger. But I could use the right to feint with, and I did, and then I let him have my left in the kisser. I put all my weight behind the punch, but it never even rocked him. He was like steel.

He roared a curse and jumped for me. I ducked him. Then I saw something sticking out of a hole in the rail. It was a belaying pin, I guess, although I don't know anything about the stuff they have on board a boat. But, anyhow, it looked something like a club, and it had a handle, and it seemed like a good weapon.

I grabbed it and smashed it down on the mate's noggin. He threw up his left hand and caught the blow on his forearm, and it never even seemed to bother him. Then, before I could bat him again, he twisted the club out of my hand and threw it across the deck. "Mutiny, huh?" he said. He slugged me on the point of the jaw and I went down and out.

When I came to, I was back in my bunk below deck, and the motion of the boat had stopped. I heard a groaning over me, and knew the little guy with the bump on his head was up there in the top bunk. He was mumbling: "Oh, my God, I've got to have fresh air! Oh, my *God!* My head hurts!"

I managed to get out of my bunk and stand on my feet. I couldn't hear anything except the little guy's moans. The boat was quiet. And, when I drew a deep breath, I couldn't smell the fresh salt tang of the ocean any more. Instead, there was an odor of stale fish, and then I heard a sort of creaking noise, like a chain rubbing against wood.

I found my way to the stairs and went up to the deck and looked around. Then I saw the schooner was anchored, and it was the anchor chain I had heard creaking against the side.

We were in a harbor, and over across the harbor I saw the lights of a city and knew it must be San Diego, because the mate had said that was where we were headed. I saw a ferry-boat crossing the harbor, all lighted up, with its windows twinkling like fireflies in the darkness.

And then I realized I had to get off the boat somehow and get back home before the cops got the idea I had jumped my bail. I looked across the water to the lights of San Diego. The harbor was still, and it had a scum of oil over the black water, and I made up my mind to slip overboard and swim to shore.

I walked toward the rail, keeping an eye peeled for the mate. I knew, if he saw me, he would make a dive for me. But he wasn't around anywhere, and I didn't spot anybody else on deck.

I started to climb over the rail and then, all of a sudden, I heard a shuffling sound behind me, and there was the little guy with the bruise on his temple. He was staring at me, with his eyes wide and empty-looking. "What are you going to do, Mister?"

I said: "Shut up, you fool. Keep your voice down. I'm going to jump overboard and swim ashore."

"But you can't do that, Mister."

"Why can't I?"

"You can't leave me here alone. That big man will kick me again. Don't leave me, Mister. Please. You've got to stay with me and help me remember something. Something I have to do."

I looked at him and felt sorry as hell for him. I knew he wasn't pulling any gag on me, but must have really lost his memory on account of that bump on his skull. He had taken one hell of a blow at some time or other, and it had scrambled his brains.

He looked so helpless it sort of made me choke up inside. "Listen, fella. There's nothing I can do for you. I tried to help you once, and that mate beat the compound cathartic out of me."

"But you're my friend. You're the only friend I've got. You can't leave me alone."

"I've got to. I've got to get ashore and get back to my home town. Otherwise I'll be in a hell of a jam."

"Then take me with you. Please."

"Hell, I can't take you with me back home, buddy. But, if you want to swim as far as shore with me, okay."

"Swim? I don't know whether I can swim. I can't remember."

"Well, it's up to you. I can't stay here all night gassing with you about it. You want to take a chance?"

"Yes, I'll take a chance. Anything to get off this boat."

"All right, then. Here I go over the side. You follow me. When you hit the water, try and swim. If you can't make it, I'll grab you and try to hold you up. I'm a pretty good swimmer."

"Thank you, Mister. You're mighty nice to me."

"Forget it, buddy." I swung one leg over the rail and then the other leg, and balanced there for a minute, and then I let go and hit the water with a splash.

There was another splash alongside me, and the little guy was in the water with me. He started to paddle away from the boat, and I saw he could swim a little, but not very good.

I stroked myself toward him and stayed alongside him, and we lit out for the lights that lined the shore across the harbor. The water was kind of cold, and I clenched my jaws to keep my teeth from chattering. But the little guy was shivering in the water, and his teeth sounded like dice rattling.

"Oh, God, my head hurts. I'm cold!" he moaned.

"Forget it, buddy. Keep swimming. That'll warm you."

Behind me I heard a shout, and I knew the mate or somebody had come to the rail of the schooner and had seen the two of us in the water. For a while I was afraid they would put a boat over the side and start after us. So I started swimming faster. And then the little guy lagged behind and started to moan again.

I swam back to him. "Put your hands on my shoulders, buddy. Just keep yourself floating, and I'll do the swimming for both of us. Make better time that way."

He did like I told him, and I struck out again. It was a tough pull, but I kept at it, and pretty soon we were at the end of a dock, and there was a rope hanging off the dock into the water. I grabbed the rope and hoisted myself up, with the little fellow still hanging on my neck. And then we were up on the dock, dripping wet.

"Come on," I said. We started sneaking along the dock, and pretty soon we got to the shore end and stepped on solid ground. We kept to the shadows so we couldn't be spotted.

When we hit the cobblestone street that ran along the waterfront, I felt easier. Just when I was drawing a deep breath and being thankful I had got this far okay, I saw something.

It was a torn piece of newspaper—the San Diego *Evening Union*. Most of the front page was there on the sidewalk, and I saw a big screamer headline across the top:

"HUNT MISSING SUSPECTS IN MASON KILLING"

Right under the headline there were two pictures. One of them was a picture of me. My heart turned a flip-flop. So the cops back home knew I had disappeared, and now they were looking for me!

Then I looked at the second picture. The caption said: "Dr. Willoughby Sebring, the dead man's medical partner, of whom no trace has yet been found."

And when I looked at that second picture, I almost had a fit of the creeping jitters. It was a picture of a little guy with grey hair, and I recognized the face.

I turned to the shrimp alongside me, and looked at him and looked at the bump on his temple, and then I looked at the newspaper picture again. I stared into the little guy's eyes and said: "So you're Dr. Willoughby Sebring!"

He said: "I don't know. Am I? The name sounds a little familiar, but I can't remember."

Fourteen

MY TONGUE FROZE UP on me for a minute when I realized the little guy with the bump on his noggin was the missing Dr. Willoughby Sebring. I couldn't talk. I couldn't ask a damned one of the million questions that flashed through my mind.

And even if I had asked them, he probably wouldn't have been able to answer. He was just standing there looking at me, with a vacant stare in his eyes, and shivering; and the water kept dripping out of his clothes and making puddles around his feet. Once he coughed a little, deep in his lungs.

After a while I gathered my wits together and grabbed hold of him and dragged him to the mouth of a dark alley behind a warehouse. "Listen, guy. You're Dr. Willoughby Sebring. Don't you remember?"

"No, I don't seem to."

"Don't you remember your partner, Dr. Carney Mason?"

"Mason? No, I don't think so. Mason's dead, isn't he?"

"Jesus Christ! Then you do remember! Why do you say Mason's dead?"

"I don't know. It just struck me he was dead, that's all. God, my head hurts me."

For a minute I had thought there was a flicker of life in his eyes, as if his brain might be coming out of its fog. But now his stare was dead and vacant again.

I shook him some more. "Listen. You're Dr. Sebring. You got to remember. Can't you think of what happened in Mason's surgery?"

"No. What happened there, Mister?"

"Mason was murdered. Did you murder him?"

"I don't know. Maybe I did. But I don't think so."

"Can't you remember a dame named Myra Holly? She was a nurse, and she worked for you and Dr. Mason. What became of her?"

"Myra Holly? How should I know what became of her? I never heard her name before, Mister. Not to my knowledge."

"Well, look. A while ago, on the boat, you said you had to get ashore because you had something important to do. What was it you had to do that was so important?"

"I don't know. I can't remember."

"Did it have anything to do with the murder of Dr. Mason?"

"I don't know."

"Did you want to go to the cops and tell them something about Mason's death?"

"I don't remember. Really I don't. All I remember is being in some stuffy place; my head hurt and I couldn't get any fresh air. Everything was all dark. After that, it's all a blank until I was on that boat with you."

"How did you get that sock on the head?"

"I don't know. But it hurts." He touched the bruise on his temple and coughed again, away down in his lungs.

And then, from the look in his eyes, I could tell I wasn't getting anywhere with him. But there was always a chance he might get a flash of memory suddenly, so I knew I had to stick with him like glue and not let him get out of my sight. I knew I had to take him back north somehow, because I had a hunch that, if he ever got his memory back, he could tell something about the two killings in Dr. Mason's surgery. The fact that his blurry brain knew Mason was dead proved to me that he knew something, if it could only be fished out.

I began to think maybe things were breaking my way at last. Here Dixie Parker had shanghaied me and put me on a boat, and, by pure dumb luck, I had found Dr. Sebring. In spite of the way Dixie had double-crossed me and drugged me, I had finally got a decent break.

But it wouldn't do me any good unless I made the most of it. I would have to duck the San Diego bulls and get Sebring back north. Then I would contact the D.A. and arrange for a brain specialist to do something for Sebring and try to bring his memory back. Maybe then Sebring would spill something that would pin the murders where they belonged and clear me.

I felt in my pocket and found my wallet and opened it, and there were two lousy, soggy dollar bills in it. That wouldn't take us back north, and I couldn't take a chance and thumb rides on the highway, for fear we might be spotted and recognized, because our pictures were on the front pages of the newspapers as wanted men.

I had to lay my hands on some dough, quick. I thought a minute, and got a sudden idea where I might pick up a few skins. It was a gamble, but it was all I could think of just then.

I turned to the little guy, who didn't suspect what I was going to do to him. I hated to do it, but it was the only way. I doubled my good left fist and clipped him on the chin. He went down.

I dragged him back along the alley and found the loading-platform of a warehouse. I pulled him up on the loading-platform and took his belt and tied his wrists together. Then I used my own belt to tie his ankles, and I stuffed my wet handkerchief in his mouth so he wouldn't wake up and make a holler and maybe bring somebody to him.

I found an empty packing-case and put him into it, and turned the open end of the packing-case against the wall of the warehouse. Nobody would ever find him there. Not until morning, anyhow. And I figured to be back after him before then.

I walked back down the alley and left him.

My wet clothes felt nasty as hell, and I kept to the shadows so nobody would notice me. If anybody saw me walking around in wet duds, it would attract attention to me, and maybe somebody would spot my face and recognize me from those newspaper pictures. And then I would be pinched by the San Diego bulls.

So I stayed in the shadows and started walking away from the wharf district. As I walked, I noticed the stars weren't shining any more, but clouds were rolling in from the direction of the ocean. All of a sudden it started to rain.

At first there were just a few big drops, but pretty soon it was a regular downpour. That was a break for me. I stood in the rain a minute and then walked on; now, if anybody saw me, they wouldn't pay any attention to my wet clothes. They would think I had got wet in the rain.

I walked on toward the business district; the streets were pretty much deserted. After a while, I found a shabby-looking drugstore and walked in and bought a tube of grease-paint for a buck. I asked the clerk to let me wash my hands, and he showed me into a dirty wash-room where there was a cracked mirror. I started working the grease-paint around my black eyes, and, when I got through, I looked more presentable. I went out again into the rain.

At the next corner, I noticed a dame standing under an awning in front of a second-hand clothing store window. I took a good squint at her, hoping she was the kind I was looking for.

She was dressed pretty gaudy, with high skirts, and a wet feather in her hat, and cheap imitation fur stringing around her neck. She was a Mex, and sort of young, and she wore a hell of a lot of powder and rouge and lipstick. Her silk stockings had ladders in them, but her legs were damned nice.

One gander told me she was just what the doctor ordered. She was a waterfront sweetie, the kind that go for the sailors off tramp steamers when they come ashore looking for a good time.

I went up to the window of the second-hand clothing store and stood there under the awning, alongside the Mex bimbo. I pretended to be looking in the window, but I took a sidewise squint at the dame and saw she was giving me the twice-over and the come-hither.

So I sort of half-turned to her and smiled a little, and she said: "Wet night, huh, boy friend?"

"Yeah. Damn wet."

"You off one of the ships, huh?"

"Yeah. Just got ashore."

"You all alone?"

"All alone."

"Lonesome?"

"I'm always lonesome."

"Know anybody here in San Diego?"

"No. Nobody."

"My name's Chiquita. What's yours?"

"They call me Duke."

"Well, Duke, a drink would go pretty good on a night like this, wouldn't it?"

I thought of the single remaining wet dollar bill in my wallet, and I knew I couldn't afford to spend it for hooch. So I said: "I don't drink."

"You don't drink?"

"No."

"What kind of guy are you, a Sunday school guy?"

"Not exactly. But I just don't drink."

"What do you do, then?"

"Oh, lots of things."

"Such as?"

"Well, I like to have fun."

She looked at me and said: "I got a room near here. Just around the next corner."

I pretended I wasn't much interested. "You look kind of skinny," I told her. "I like my dames to have some meat on 'em."

She pulled her skirt up above her knees. She had her stockings rolled. "Look. Not bad, huh, sailor?"

"No. Not so bad. Legs don't mean very much to me."

She looked up and down the street to see if anybody was coming. Nobody was. She opened her jacket and unbuttoned her shirtwaist a little way so I could see her breasts nestling in the cheap mesh cups of a brassiere. She ran her fingers in one of the mesh cups and popped her left breast out of it for a second, and then she pulled her jacket together again. "How you like that, huh, sailor?"

"I like it okay."

"I'm built, ain't I? I'm firm, don't you think?"

"Yeah, you're built, all right. You're plenty firm."

"Well, come on, then. What are we waiting for?"

I slipped my hand through the crook of her arm. "Okay, sister."

Fifteen

WE WALKED around the corner and came to a door. The door led to a narrow stairway up over a fish market that was closed for the night. The stairs were dirty, and the hallway smelled of fish and Lysol mixed together. There was a gas light burning at the head of the stairs in a filthy red globe.

The Mex dame said: "Come on, honey. I live up here."

"All right. I'm with you."

We went up the stairs, which creaked under my feet. The Mex dame went up ahead of me, and I could see her hips swaying on a line with my eyes. They were pretty nice.

We came to a room. She unlocked the door, and we went inside. She struck a match to a gas light over the bed, and then she lit a little gas fire heater on the other side of the room. She took off her hat and jacket and the wet fur-piece and threw them on a chair in the corner.

I noticed a string running from one wall to the other, near the gas fire. I said: "How about letting me hang my coat near the fire, sister? It's plenty wet."

"Sure. Go ahead. Help yourself, big boy. You can take off as much as you want to."

But all I took off was my coat, because, when the time came, I wanted to be dressed, so I could lam in a hurry.

While I was taking off my coat, she unfastened her skirt and dropped it around her ankles and stepped out of it. Then she kicked off her soggy, high-heeled shoes and slipped out of her shirt-waist, and I saw she wasn't wearing anything except the mesh-net brassiere and cheap rayon step-ins. The lace edges of the step-ins were torn.

She smiled and walked toward me. "Well, big boy?"

I sat on the edge of the bed, and pulled her down alongside me, and mauled her a little and unfastened her brassiere. She was wearing a hell of a lot of strong, cheap perfume, but her skin was smooth and soft.

She looked at me. "You don't act as if you was very interested. You got something on your mind, maybe?"

"No," I told her. But I was lying. I was thinking of Sebring, all tied up in that packing-case behind that warehouse. I was hoping to God he wouldn't get away. I had a hunch he was going to help me get out from under the Mason murder rap if I could ever get him back north with me.

The Mex wren said: "How about giving me some dough, sailor, and then let's make love? Huh?"

I got up and went over to where my coat was hanging. I pulled out my wallet and dug out the water-soaked one-buck note. I handed it to her.

"That all you got, big boy?" she asked. She looked disappointed.

"Yeah." I showed her my empty wallet.

"Well, okay." She took the wet dollar and went to a closet door and opened it. I watched her out of the tail of my eye, although I pretended I wasn't looking.

I saw her pick up an old slipper from the closet and stuff the buck into the toe. The slipper looked all puffed out, and I knew there must be other money in it. But it wasn't time for me to make my play yet.

The Mex cutie put the slipper back in the closet, and then came over to me and stood in front of me at the edge of the bed, like a strip-tease girl in a burlesque show. Her breasts jiggled behind the unfastened brassiere.

I grabbed her in my arms and pulled her on the bed and leaned over her. I sure as hell hated what I was going to do to her, but there was no other way. I pretended I was going to slip my arm around her bare waist and lift her up toward me and kiss her. But when she held up her mouth to be kissed, I punched her square on the button with my left fist.

She went out like a light.

I made sure she was unconscious. Then I covered her up with the blanket of the bed, because, after all, I'm not a complete heel, and I didn't want her to lie there and maybe catch cold.

After I covered her, I went to the closet and felt around until I found that slipper she used for a bank. I dug my fingers into the toe of the slipper and felt a wad of crumpled bills. I pulled them out and took enough time to straighten them and count them. There were seven ones, a two and a five.

I turned down the gas light and left the fire burning a little to keep the room warm, and then I started to go out. But I stopped. I hated to leave the Mex dame broke, even though I intended to send this back tomorrow, maybe. There was a chance she wouldn't feel like working tomorrow, I thought, after that paste on the jaw I just gave her.

So I peeled four ones off the roll, including the wet bill I had given her, and I stuffed the four bucks in the toe of her slipper and put it back in the closet. That still left me ten, which I figured would be enough.

I took one last look at the cutie on the bed, and then I went out and closed the door of the room after me.

Downstairs on the street, the first guy I saw was a harness bull patrolling his beat and swinging his locust. I ducked into and alley and waited until he went past. When I was sure he was gone and hadn't spotted me, I sneaked out of the alley and started for the waterfront.

It was still drizzling, and nobody was on the streets at that late hour, anyhow. So I was pretty sure I didn't stand much chance of being seen and picked up. But, just the same, I kept to the shadows and went down alleys wherever I could. That was safest.

After a while, I came to the wharf district and got my bearings. I walked along until I came to the warehouse where I had left Sebring. I ducked into the alley behind the warehouse and came to the loading-platform. I climbed up and went to the packing-case where I had put the little guy.

I pulled the packing-case away from the wall, and it felt sort of light. Then I swung the case around, and I felt my throat tighten.

"Jesus Christ!" I whispered.

Dr. Sebring was gone.

Sixteen

IT KNOCKED ME all in a heap for a minute. I didn't know which way to turn. Then, up ahead of me, I noticed a dim light. It was shining from a rear window in the warehouse. I went toward it and, when I got near it, I saw that it was open a crack, and I could hear voices inside.

I sneaked up and peeped in, and my heart started hammering. There, on a chair inside a little room, was Dr. Sebring. He was looking up at a guy in corduroy pants and sweater. The guy had a badge pinned to his sweater and wore a cap that said: "WATCHMAN." The watchman had a gat in one hand and a flashlight in the other. He was flashing the light in Sebring's empty-looking eyes and asking questions. "How did you get in that packing-case?"

"I don't quite remember," Sebring said. Then he coughed, down deep in his lungs. "Oh, God my head hurts. Please let me out of here. I've got to get some fresh air."

"Not yet you don't get out of here, buddy. First you'll tell me a few things. You say you don't know how you come to be in that box, all tied up?"

"No. I don't remember. Wait a minute. I think I remember. I was with a man who has two teeth missing in front. I think he hit me and tied me up and put me in that box. But I'm not sure."

"A guy with two teeth out, huh? What was his name?"

"I don't know."

"Two teeth out—Hm-m-m-m." The watchman's eyes suddenly widened.

"Say—I know you! I seen your picture tonight in the *Evening Union*. Your name's Sebring—Dr. Willoughby Sebring! You're wanted on the Mason murder up north!"

"Am I? I didn't know that."

"And the guy with two teeth out—I remember readin' about him, too. He's supposed to be the one that bumped this Dr. Mason and some broad. The paper gave a description of him and said he had two teeth out in front. They was knocked out in a brawl, or something. His name is Duke Pizzatello! Is that the guy that tied you up?"

"I don't know, really."

"Well, you know you're Dr. Willoughby Sebring, don't you?"

"No. But I seem to remember someone telling me I was. Do you really think my name's Sebring?"

"Hell, I *know* it! Listen—I'm goin' back through the warehouse and phone for the cops. Maybe I'll get a reward."

"A reward?"

"Yeah." The watchman leaned over and picked up the two belts I had used to tie Sebring in the first place, when I'd left him in that packing-box.

He wrapped one of the belts around the little guy's wrists and the other one around his ankles. Then he took his flashlight with him and walked out of the room and left everything all dark.

Outside the window, I waited until I heard the watchman's footsteps fade off. I heard Sebring cough, deep in his chest, and sort of groan: "Oh, God! I've got to get some fresh air. Oh, *God!* My head hurts!"

I backed off from the window and gathered my muscles and smashed at the glass sidewise, with my shoulders. The pane crashed and splintered and tinkled on the floor, making a hell of a lot of racket. I dived into the room and found the little guy and picked him up. I lifted him and shoved him through the window out onto the loading platform.

Then I scrambled out after him. Back in the warehouse, I heard the watchman yelling and running toward us. I unfastened the belts from around Sebring's ankles and wrists and said: "Come on, buddy. Let's get going."

"Where are we going?"

"Never mind. Start running, for Christ's sake." I grabbed his arm and started dragging him, and he broke into a wavering trot alongside me. We got to the end of the platform and jumped down and started out the alley.

Behind us, I heard the watchman run out on the platform. He yelled: "Halt, in the name of the law!"

"Nuts!" I whispered under my breath, and kept going.

"Halt, or I'll shoot!"

I didn't care how much the watchman shot. He couldn't see us in that dark alley, anyhow. I heard his roscoe go off with a hell of a roar, and a slug whistled past me, over my head. I steered Sebring by his elbow out of the alley and we pelted down the street.

He was panting and wheezing in this throat. "I can't run any more, Mister. I'm tired. My head hurts."

"You got to run, buddy. Do you want to go to jail?"

"No. Why should I go to jail?"

"Because the cops think you're a murderer, that's why."

"Why should they think that? I don't remember murdering anyone."

"Hell, you don't remember anything. Come on." I pulled him along.

He dragged back again. "Wait a minute. You hit me and tied me up and put me in that box, didn't you?"

I didn't want trouble with him just then, so I said: "Not me. Your brain's playing you tricks."

"That's queer. I thought you were the one. But no, you can't be. I was hit and put into a little space last night or the night before, not tonight. And it wasn't you who did it."

I caught my breath. Sebring was beginning to remember something! "Who hit you?" I asked.

"It's funny. I don't remember."

"Try and think. And keep on running while you're thinking."

"It's all so mixed up. My head hurts, too. But it seems as if someone hit me on the head and put me in a little place like a closet. It seems as if that happened to me a couple of nights ago. I can't remember much after that. But it's all mixed up with tonight. I keep thinking it was you who hit me and tied me up and put me in a little place like a packing-box. Why is everything so mixed up, Mister?"

"I don't know. Come on, keep going." By that time we were out of the warehouse district, and it was raining harder than ever. All of a sudden I saw a garage with an open front and a sign on it that said: "U-DRIVE."

"In here, buddy!" I said to the little guy. I dragged him down to a walk, and we stepped into the garage. A sleepy-looking young fellow came toward us.

I said: "Buddy, I want to rent a car. A little car."

"A Ford, maybe?"

"Yeah, that'll do."

The garage guy looked me over. My clothes were plenty wet and mussed, and I guess I didn't look so hot. Neither did Sebring. I could tell the garage kid wasn't very impressed with us.

Then I got an idea. I remembered I had my private detective badge pinned to a leather flap in my wallet. So I dragged out the wallet and flashed the tin. "It's police business, fella. And here's ten bucks deposit on the jaloppy." I shoved out the ten skins I had swiped from that Mex dame.

The kid softened up. "Okay, Mister." He took the ten clams and went to the rear of the garage. He got into a Model A coupé and stepped on the starter. The motor coughed and caught on, and it sounded nice and smooth and tight.

The kid drove the coupé up front, then got out and went into his office. He filled out a couple of forms for me to sign, and I scrawled the first name I could think of on the dotted line. Then I said: "Gas in that flivver, buddy?"

"Half a tank full."

"Better fill it up all the way."

"We never put more than half a tank full in our rent cars, Mister."

"I don't give a damn what you usually do. Fill it up and make it snappy. I haven't got all night. I told you this was police business. I'm after a guy who shot the front tires off my own car, and I've got to have another crate right away—with gas in it."

"Well, all right."

The kid got into the coupé and rolled it to a gas pump. He got out and shoved the nozzle of the gas hose into the tank and started working the handle of the pump back and forth. I thought it would take him forever, and I was getting jittery. Maybe that warehouse watchman had called the cops by this time, and the dragnet would be out for me and Dr. Sebring.

But pretty soon the coupé's tank was full and a little gas spilled over. The kid pulled the hose nozzle out and put the tank cap on and said: "There you are, Mister."

"Thanks, buddy."

I made Sebring get into the car, and then I climbed in alongside him and sat under the steering-wheel. I slipped into gear and switched on the headlights and drove out of the garage. I headed through the darkest streets I could find, but I didn't drive too fast, for fear some speed-bull would light out after me.

Pretty soon we got to the outskirts of San Diego, and I boosted the speed a little. Sebring said: "Where are you taking me, Mister?"

"Up north," I told him.

"What for?" he asked me, coughing in his chest.

I said: "Never mind. You'll find out when the time comes."

Seventeen

SEBRING WAS QUIET for a while after that. As we went farther out of town, I built the coupé's speed up to around fifty. The rain was coming down pretty hard. I kept the windshield wiper wagging like a dog's tail and stared ahead, through the clear space in the glass, into the black night. Every now and then I squinted into the rear-view mirror to make sure we weren't being followed.

Pretty soon we were on the road that runs along the ocean shore, and there weren't very many other cars on the highway. After maybe fifteen minutes, Sebring said: "Mister, do you mind if I roll down the window on this side? I've got to have some fresh air. My head hurts."

"You'll get wet. The rain will blow in on you."

"I'm already wet, Mister. I'm soaked through." He coughed, and I could feel him shivering beside me.

I said: "That's a bad cough, buddy. Maybe you took cold when we jumped off that boat."

"Yes. I think I did. I think my temperature is above normal. My respiration rate is too fast, too. Pneumococcus, probably."

"Pneumococcus? What's that?"

"Pneumonia germs."

I took a quick sidewise gander at him. That was doctor talk. Maybe he was beginning to remember he was Dr. Willoughby Sebring! My heart began to thump. "Listen, buddy. Do you know your name now?"

"No, I don't remember it. But you said I was Dr. Sebring, didn't you?"

"Yeah. That's who you are, all right."

"I wish I could remember something about myself. What's your name, Mister?"

"Me? I'm Duke Pizzatello."

"Pizzatello. That's an odd name."

"I'm Italian."

"Of course. Look, Mr. Pizzatello. Where did you say you were taking me?"

"Up north."

"What for?"

"To talk to the cops."

"The police? Why should I talk to the police?"

"To tell them what you know about the killing of your partner, Dr. Mason."

"Do I know anything about that?"

"Sure you do. Try and remember." Of course I wasn't sure he knew anything, but I had a hunch he did, and I was hoping to hell I could make his brains work out of their fog if I kept plugging away at him.

He said: "I don't remember anything much. When I saw Mason and that woman being killed, somebody hit me on the head and put me in a little place like a closet, and then everything is blank."

I almost let the coupé skid off the road. "Jesus! You saw Mason and the dame being croaked?"

His voice got blurry again. "I don't know. Is that what I said?"

"Sure you said it. Just now. For the love of Christ, pull yourself together. Tell me what you know!"

"But I don't know anything. I can't remember. Why do you keep asking me questions, Mr. Pizzatello?"

"God—I got to ask you questions! The police think maybe I'm the guy that bumped Mason and the dame."

"Well, didn't you?"

"No! Goddam it, no!"

"But you hit me over the head and put me in that little place, didn't you?"

I began to curse myself for biffing him and tying him in that packing-case. The way his twisted brain was working, he had tonight mixed up with the night of the murder. If he kept thinking along those lines, he might come out and say I was the murderer, and then my goose would be cooked plenty.

From what he had already spilled to me, I began to get a picture of what must have happened the night of the killings. He must have walked into Mason's surgery and seen Mason and the dame being croaked. Then the murderer must have spotted him, and biffed him on the temple and stuffed him in a closet to get him out of the way while finishing up the job of slicing the dead dame into shreds.

The blow must have scrambled Sebring's brains plenty. But he had probably come to and got out of the closet and sneaked away, looking for fresh air. I could imagine how the murderer must have felt, going back to the closet to drag Sebring out and finish him, only to find that he had lammed.

But the hell of it was—Sebring now had everything all mixed up. He was confusing the night of the murders with tonight in his mind—all because I had popped him and stuffed him in that packing-case while I went out looking for money to get him back north. It was just my damned lousy luck to do something to him that was almost exactly like what had happened to him the night of the killings.

I knew I had to work on him and try to get the two nights separated in his mind. I said: "Listen, Dr. Sebring. You say you saw Mason and a woman being killed, and then the murderer hit you because you witnessed the crime."

"Did I say that?"

"Yeah. Well, tell me. Was the murderer a man or a woman?"

"I don't know. I don't remember anything about it. Oh, God, my head hurts!" He coughed and wheezed down in his lungs, and shivered against me, while the rain pelted in on him through the open window of the coupé on his side.

I tried another question. "The woman who was murdered—was she your nurse, Myra Holly?"

"No."

"Well, then, who was she?"

"Who was who?"

I gritted my teeth. He was going off into a fog again. I
said: "Who was the dame that got killed and was all carved
up?"

"I don't know. I don't remember anything about it.
Sometimes I think I'm about to remember something, but
then it all slips away, because my head hurts so badly."

"Do you know Carney Mason's wife? Nelia Mason? A
red-haired dame with funny eyes like a cat?"

"No. I don't know her."

"Was it Mrs. Mason that did the killing?"

"I don't remember."

"Well, do you remember Myra Holly?"

"Myra Holly? That sounds familiar. She's very pretty,
isn't she? I was in love with her."

I caught my breath. His thoughts were clearing up
again! "So you were in love with Myra Holly, huh? You
mean you played around with her? There was something
doing between you two?"

"Yes. That's why my wife divorced me, on account of
Myra Holly."

"Oh. So you're divorced, are you?"

"Of course. Everybody knows that."

I said: "Did Dr. Mason ever get gay with Myra Holly?"

"Yes, damn him!"

"You fought with Mason about her?"

"Plenty. Say, listen. You're asking me too many questions. If you don't look out, I'll do the same thing to you
that I did to Mason and Myra Holly! I'll kill you and cut
you to pieces with a scalpel!" Then he began to cough, and
laugh at the top of his voice like a crazy man, and saliva
drooled down out of his lips, and he squirmed in the seat
alongside me.

I almost lost my hold on the wheel. God almighty! Sebring had just admitted he was the murderer! And he had also admitted that the carved-up dame was the missing nurse, Myra Holly!

And now he was laughing at the top of his lungs and acting as if he had gone completely cuckoo. I felt a little cuckoo myself. First Sebring had said he'd witnessed the murders, and now he said he had done them himself. There was froth at his mouth, and he was sticking his head out the side of the car so that the rain would beat down on his face. I began to feel scared. It's a hell of a funny sensation to be driving along with a maniac beside you. Any minute, I figured, Sebring would get violent and grab for the wheel and maybe put us in the ditch.

He was getting more delirious by the second. I reached over and grabbed him and hauled him back so his head wasn't out the window any more.

"For Christ's sake, get quiet!" I yelled at him. "You goddam loon!"

Then, all of a sudden, I saw headlights behind me, a sedan pulled around me and came up even. I looked and saw it was a white sedan with the California state emblem on its door, and with a red spotlight, which meant it was a cop car. Somebody inside the sedan turned the red spotlight around and blazed it at me.

The patrol car was nosing me over to the side of the road, and a uniformed copper stuck out his head and yelled: "Haul up, buddy. I want to talk to you."

Eighteen

I JAMMED DOWN on my brakes. A cold chill skittered the length of my backbone. I figured that that goddam night watchman back at the warehouse in San Diego had put in a beef to the bulls, and the coppers had traced me to the U-Drive garage and sent out a radio call to all highway patrols, and now I was pinched.

I rolled the coupé window all the way down on my side, and looked out at the state copper in the white sedan. "You want to talk to me?"

"Yeah. You heading all the way north?"

I nodded, wondering what was coming.

"Well, part of the cliff has been washed down on the road by rain, two miles ahead. There ain't been time to put out red lanterns yet, so be careful. Drive slow, because it'll be a one-way road through the narrow part where the rock-slide was."

"Is that all?"

"Yeah, that's all."

I could almost have got out and kissed that cop. So I wasn't pinched, after all! I took a deep breath and said: "Okay, Captain. Thanks a lot for telling me."

"That's all right. You're welcome, buddy."

I slipped into gear and started out again, and my pulse was hammering like hell and my palms were wet and clammy. I got into high, and didn't drive any faster than thirty, and in my rear-view mirror I saw the cop car turning around and going back toward San Diego. I felt Sebring leaning against me, sort of still, and I said to him: "Jesus, that was a narrow squeak."

He didn't answer me. I took a quick look at him; his eyes were closed and his jaw hung open and he was breathing fast and jerky. I reached up and felt his cheek, and it was hot, like he was on fire inside. He was burning up with fever, and I knew he must be on the edge of pneumonia, if he didn't already have it.

It scared me, him passing out that way. I knew I had to get him somewhere, and dry him out, and maybe give him some medicine or have a doctor for him. I began to worry for fear he might die on me before I could get a brain specialist to bring his memory back so he could spill what he knew.

While I drove, I tried to piece things together from what he had said. For one thing, he had told me his wife had divorced him on account of his playing around with Myra Holly. All of a sudden it struck me I had a new suspect: Sebring's divorced wife.

Suppose she was a crazy jealous dame, and had gone to the surgery the night of the murders and caught Sebring with the nurse? In that case, she might have biffed Sebring cold, and then killed Myra Holly and carved her up. Then maybe Dr. Mason walked in and caught her, and she'd shot him to keep him from talking. Then maybe she went in to find her husband where she had stuffed him in a closet, but he had got away in the meantime, with his brains scrambled.

That might explain why Sebring had just confessed to me that he was the murderer himself. Maybe he had got a flash of memory and realized his divorced wife was the killer; and maybe he still cared enough for her not to want her to go to the gallows. So maybe he was fronting for her by taking the blame on his own shoulders.

It was just about dawn when I finally got to my own apartment. I drove the rented jaloppy into the basement garage and slapped Sebring across the face to wake him up. He opened his eyes, and they were sort of glazed, and he didn't know where he was or what had happened to him during the night. His memory was gone again.

He groaned: "I've got to have fresh air. Oh, God, my head hurts!" He coughed a rasping cough that seemed to tear his lungs all to shreds.

There was a back stairway inside the basement garage, and I took him to it and carried him upstairs to my apartment on the third floor. I took out my key, and opened the door, and lifted Sebring inside and locked the door after us.

I carried him to my bedroom and stripped off his wet duds. I put pajamas on him and covered him with a lot of blankets on my bed and made him drink a big slug of rye. He dropped off to sleep, breathing fast and heavy.

The sun was just coming up, and my eyes felt like lead. I was fagged. I got my alarm clock, set it for eight A.M. and took it into the living room. I threw myself on the couch and was asleep like a shot. It didn't seem five minutes until that damned alarm clock jangled and woke me up.

I got up and had a drink to steady myself. Then I went to my phone and dialed the Kohlar detective agency. I recognized Dixie Parker's voice saying: "Hello?"

"Let me talk to Steve Kohlar, please," I said. I tried to disguise my voice so she wouldn't tab me, because I didn't trust her—after the way she had doped me and shanghaied me.

"He isn't in," she said. "But Mr. Joseph Kohlar is here."

I started to say: "Never mind," because it made me jittery to talk to Joe Kohlar ever since the night I'd gone out with Gertie, his wife. I felt like a heel every time I passed a dozen words with him.

But before I could tell Dixie not to call Joe, he came on the wire. "Yes?"

"Listen, Joe. This is Duke Pizzatello."

"Well, well!" His voice sounded cold and harsh.

"Yeah," I said. "I'm back in my apartment. I've got to talk with Steve. Where can I reach him?"

"I don't know. He should be on his way down here to

the office right now. What do you want to talk to him about?"

Well, I couldn't very well make any excuses, because, after all, Joe was my boss, the same as Steve. So I said: "Listen. I've got Dr. Willoughby Sebring here in my joint with me."

"The hell!"

"Yeah. He's lost his memory, but he had a couple of flashes of sense while I was bringing him here. He either knows who croaked Mason and that dame, or else he did it himself!"

"I'll be damned!"

"Yeah. That's why I wanted to talk with Steve. I need advice. What do you think I ought to do?"

"Any half-wit ought to know the answer to that one!" Joe snapped, sort of surly. "Take him to the district attorney, of course."

"I can't. Sebring's sick. I think it's pneumonia. I can't move him out of my apartment. He might die."

"Then phone the D.A. and have him come to your place."

"Okay, Joe. Thanks. That's what I'll do. Has anything new developed in the Mason case while I been gone?"

"No. Nothing new. The cops are looking for you. I suppose you realize that."

"Yeah, I figured they would be." I didn't want to bother telling him all that had happened to me. It could wait. So I said: "Well, I'll be seeing you, Joe," and hung up.

I waited a minute, and then started to call the district attorney's office. But before I could find the number in the phone book, my telephone rang. I figured maybe it was Joe Kohlar calling me back for something or other. So I answered the phone. "Hello?"

"Duke, is that you?"

It was Dixie Parker's voice.

I started to hang up on her, but she began talking fast. "Listen, Duke. Don't hang up on me. I've got just a minute. Steve just came in and wants me to take some dictation.

But look: I plugged in on Joe's line when you called, and I heard everything you said to him."

"So what?"

"Don't be sore at me, Wop. I can explain the things I did. You remember you were in my apartment when I got a phone call?"

"Yeah. You said it was your beauty parlor. You lied."

"Sure. I admit I lied. The message I got was that Nelia Mason had put in a complaint to the police after you tried to beat her up. The cops were looking for you on an assault charge. I knew, if I told you, you wouldn't have sense enough to get out of sight and stay out of sight. So I drugged you and dragged you down to my car and started driving around, wondering where to hide you. I wound up in San Pedro, along the wharves, and, all of a sudden, I saw a little grey-haired man on one of the boats."

"You mean Dr. Sebring?"

"I thought that's who it was, but I wasn't sure. So I bribed the mate of the boat to take you aboard. That got you out of the way of the cops for a while, and I knew, if the grey-haired man really was Dr. Sebring, you'd find it out when you came to."

"How the hell would I find it out when I never saw the bird before?"

"Well, you *did* find it out, Duke."

"Yeah, by accident." I put a sneer in my voice.

"Listen, Wop. You're still sore at me, aren't you?"

"Plenty."

"I'm coming up to see you," Dixie said.

"What for?"

"To have a talk with you."

"That won't do any good."

"I'm coming, anyhow." She hung up.

I waited a minute, and then dialed City Hall. "Give me District Attorney Terhune."

In a moment, I heard a voice saying: "Terhune speaking."

"Hello. This is Duke Pizzatello."

"What?"

"Yeah. Listen. I didn't jump my bail, Mr. Terhune. I was out on a hot trail. Now I got somebody in my apartment you'll want to see."

"Who is it?"

"Dr. Willoughby Sebring—that's who."

"The devil you say!"

"Yeah. But something's wrong with his brain. He can't remember anything much."

"Amnesia?"

"I guess that's what you call it. He's got a bad bump on his head, and his brains are scrambled. But he had a couple of flashes of memory while I was bringing him here, and he spilled something to me. He either saw Mason and that broad being croaked, or else he did it himself."

"Good Lord! I'll send some men to get him right away."

"No. You can't move him. He's sick. I think it's pneumonia. You'll have to come here if you want to question him. Bring a brain doctor with you, and I guess you'd better bring a regular doctor, too."

"All right. I'll do that."

Then I got a sudden idea. I said: "Listen, Mr. Terhune. Why don't you call up Nelia Mason and get her to come with you? And maybe you can get hold of Sebring's divorced wife. Bring her if you can. Maybe, when Sebring sees somebody he knows, his memory will come back."

"Good idea, Pizzatello. I'll phone both those women at once and have them meet me at your place. You wait where you are. Don't let Sebring out of your sight—understand? I'll be right over as soon as I can pick up a medico and an alienist."

I hung up, and then I heard a sound in my bedroom. I ran in, and Sebring had got out of bed and had raised the window and was leaning away out. "I've got to have fresh air!" he was moaning.

I grabbed him quick. "You want to fall out and bust your neck?" I put him back in bed, and gave him another stiff jorum of rye, and he went to sleep again. I tore a sheet into strips and tied his legs to the foot of the bed for safety.

While I was doing it, I heard somebody fumbling at my front door. I went to see who it was, but all I found was a letter sticking through the slot.

I picked up the letter and recognized the handwriting. It was from Gertie Kohlar, postmarked Fresno.

Nineteen

I GOT A FUNNY FEELING when I saw the handwriting on the envelope, because I had almost forgotten Gertie after the screwy things that had happened to me during the past twenty-four hours.

I ripped open the letter. There was a single sheet of paper inside, with both sides written on, in pencil:

> "Dear Duke—
>
> Well, I have made all the arrangements for that operation. But the doctor wants dough on the line, so you will have to send me some cash right away.
>
> I know you won't have any trouble sending me the money, because I remember, the night before I left to come up here, I came to see you, and you said some woman wanted her husband croaked and offered you the job, but you turned it down.
>
> Well, I been reading the papers, and I see you are in a jam over a killing but are out on bail, so I guess you must of went through with the dame's proposition. So send me some dough and don't tell me you ain't got it, because I know you must of got paid for that bump-off. Duke, if you throw me down, I will get plenty even. How would you like me to tell the cops how you was offered money to croak Dr. Mason?
>
> But of course I won't spill anything, because I know you will send me some dough right away in care of general delivery, Fresno.
>
> Gertie."

When I got through reading that letter, my knees were weak. I had forgotten that Gertie had come to me the evening of the murders and I'd spilled my guts to her. Now she thought I had croaked Mason and his broad and, unless I sent her some cash, she would make things plenty hot for me. Her testimony, piled on top of my two slugs in Mason's cork leg, would cook my goose.

So I had to get hold of some geetus to keep Gertie from throwing me in the soup. I dug around in my bureau and found an old solid gold pocket watch, and some studs with chip diamonds in them, and an imitation emerald stickpin set in solid gold that I didn't wear any more, on account of stickpins being out of style. I gathered all that junk together and put my wrist-watch with it, and then I took a look at the bed to make sure Sebring was still asleep.

His eyes were closed, and he was breathing hard. I covered him with the blankets and saw that his legs were tied tight to the foot of the bed. Then I put on my hat and coat and went out.

There was a hock-shop in the next block. I went there and dumped all that jewelry junk on the counter. "How much for this stuff, Uncle?"

He fumbled around for a while, and then said: "I give you a hundred dollars."

"Suits me."

He counted out ten tens and shoved them at me. Then I went out. I had to get back to my place and write a letter to Gertie and enclose the money and mail it before people started busting in. Pretty soon I was expecting Dixie Parker, and the district attorney, and some doctors, and Nelia Mason and the divorced Mrs. Sebring. I had to get the letter off before they all got to my flat.

I ran the whole two blocks back from the hock-shop and, when I got to my apartment building, I noticed Dixie's little car standing outside. Then, just as I passed the mouth of the alley alongside the building, Dixie came running out of the alley and grabbed me. She looked pale.

"Duke!"

"Hello. What's up?"

"Listen. Come here in the alley with me a minute."

"Why?"

"I've got something to show you."

I held back, because I didn't trust her. She might have somebody waiting in the alley to slug me, or something. I said: "What's it all about? You're shaking to beat hell."

"You'll shake, too, when you see what I'm going to show you. Listen, Wop. Just as I parked my car here a minute ago, I heard a scream, and then a sort of squishy bump. It was in the alley. Come on—come look for yourself."

I went with her into the alley. Then I felt as if somebody had landed a haymaker in my guts.

There in the alley was a sprawled shape, all bloody and smashed to hell. It was a man with grey hair, and his head was cracked open, and his brains were splattered all over the cement of the alley. It didn't take two looks to see he was dead.

He was Dr. Willoughby Sebring—what was left of him.

Twenty

I FELT SICK, because I had been depending on Sebring to clear me of the Mason murder rap. I'd been hoping some way could be found to make him remember what happened the night of the killings. But there was no chance of unscrambling his brains now. They were smeared all over the cement paving of the alley. Falling or jumping out my bedroom window, he had landed on his noggin, and that was the end of Dr. Willoughby Sebring. It looked like it might be the end of me, too.

But that wasn't the only reason I felt queasy. Somehow, I had taken a shine to the little guy. He had been so damned sick and weak and helpless, and had depended on me so much, that I couldn't help liking him. And now he was dead.

I said: "God almighty! This is my fault!"

"Your fault, Duke?"

"Yeah. He kept having a nutty idea he needed fresh air. He got away from me once, in my bedroom, and went to the window and leaned away out. I had to drag him back. He didn't know what he was doing. I shouldn't have left him." I started for the entrance to my apartment house to go upstairs and phone the cops.

Dixie held my arm and pulled me toward her little car. "Duke—don't go upstairs. Please. You've got to come with me."

"Why do I?"

"Listen. The police will find Sebring's body soon enough. And, when they do, they'll accuse you of murdering him. They already think you killed Mason and the carved-up woman."

"Yeah. I know."

"Well, when they find Sebring dead, too, they'll think maybe you killed him also. Because maybe he knew too much about you."

"That's crazy. Why would I bring Sebring here, and phone the D.A. to get a brain doctor to make him remember what happened the night of the murders, if I thought he might spill something to put me in the grease? That don't make sense, babe."

"Maybe not. But the point is: here's another death at your doorstep. When it's discovered, you'll be taken into custody as a material witness. That's the least can happen to you." Dixie was talking fast and desperate.

She was probably right, I thought. I didn't figure I'd be accused of tossing Sebring out my bedroom window, but I would certainly be held for questioning. And I couldn't afford to let that happen, because I needed my freedom now more than ever so I could do some fast investigating. With Sebring dead, I couldn't count on him helping me beat my murder rap. Whatever he might have known was wiped out, and I was now strictly on my own.

Any minute the D.A. would be showing up, with his dicks and his doctors and Nelia Mason and Mrs. Sebring. So it was probably best for me to lam while I still had the chance.

I let Dixie pull me to her car, and I got in alongside her. She gunned the motor, and we went away from there in a hell of a rush. My mind kept going back to poor little Sebring, stretched out dead in the alley under my bedroom window. "I shouldn't have left him alone!"

"Then why did you?"

"I had to. I had to go around to a hock-shop and get some dough on some jewelry and junk."

"Money? What for?"

"To send to Gertie Kohlar in Fresno. I got another letter from her a while ago."

"I should think you'd forget her for a while, considering the jam you're in."

"Yeah? That's where you're haywire, babe. Gertie came to me the evening of the murders and told me she was in trouble and needed dough. Like a goddam fool, I told her about some dame wanting her husband croaked and how I had turned the job down."

"Good lord, Wop!"

"Yeah. And in her letter that I got just now, she says she figures I really went ahead with the deal. She's been reading the papers in Fresno, and knows all about how I been arrested for the Mason murders. So she figures I'm really guilty."

"And now she's blackmailing you, eh?"

"Maybe you might call it that. She hinted, if I didn't kick in with some dough, she'd go to the cops and squeal about me having a proposition to croak Dr. Mason. That would put my fanny in a sling, and I don't mean maybe."

"Nice girl—Gertie Kohlar!"

"All dames are the balls."

"Including me?"

"Yeah, including you."

"You don't trust me, do you, Wop?"

"Not any too much, babe. I'm getting so I don't trust anybody."

Dixie looked at me quick, out of the corner of her eye, while she drove. "Maybe you think I sneaked up to your apartment just now while you were out and threw Dr. Sebring out your window. Maybe you think I murdered Mason and that woman, night before last."

"That's an idea. I hadn't thought of that." Of course I figured she was kidding, because why would Dixie have any reason for bumping Mason—or anybody else, for that matter? Besides, nobody had tossed Willoughby Sebring out my window. He had fallen of his own accord. It just had to be that way.

But I was still half sore at Dixie on account of the screwy things she had done to me. Her actions had been plenty queer—ever since she'd caught me trying to beat

Mrs. Mason up. Over the hum of her jaloppy's motor, I said: "Babe, who the hell are you fronting for?"

"Oh, damn you, Duke, if I'm fronting for anyone, it's you!"

"You mean you think I'm the guy that killed Mason and his broad?"

"I didn't say that. But there's a lot of evidence pointing your way."

"Jesus, babe, I thought I explained all that stuff to you."

"You did. But I don't have to believe you, do I?"

"You got to. You know I been leveling with you. I been leveling with you more than you been leveling with me."

"Have you?"

"Yeah. Next thing I know, you'll be telling me *I* tossed Sebring out of my window!"

"Well, did you?"

"Oh, cut it out, for cripe's sake. You saw me running back from the hock-shop at the same time he fell in the alley. How could I be two places at once? I'm not twins."

"Sometimes I wish you were. Maybe I'd like the other twin better." All of a sudden she slapped on her brakes and parked her car, and I saw we were outside a third-rate hotel.

I said: "Where are we going now?"

"We're going in this hotel and hide you out for a while."

"What for?"

"To keep you from being picked up by the cops and taken back into custody. And I'm staying with you, to see you don't sneak out and put your foot in more trouble."

"You're going with me in the hotel?"

"Yes. We'll register as man and wife, and we'll stay until dark, anyhow."

"Man and wife, huh?"

She looked at me sort of funny. "Well, why not?"

Twenty-one

I SAID: "OKAY, BABE. Lend me a little jack so I can pay for the room. I don't want to break this century I got in the hock-shop to send to Gertie."

She slipped me a fin, and we went into the hotel, and I registered as Mr. and Mrs. John Jones. The clerk didn't say anything, but just grinned, when he saw we didn't have any luggage.

Upstairs in the bedroom, Dixie took off her hat and patted back her yellow hair, while I slipped out of my coat and vest and kicked off my shoes and threw myself across the bed. I was plenty tired, seeing that I hadn't had much sleep, and my ribs were sore from the pounding I had taken down at the jail night before last, and my busted finger ached in its splint.

Dixie sat down in a chair and took a cigarette out of her handbag and lit it. She said: "Well, Wop. I wonder how much longer this is going to keep up."

"How long what is going to keep up?"

"You ducking the cops and me helping you do it. And, all the time, the real murderer running around loose."

"Oh. So you don't really think I bumped Mason and his broad, huh?"

"No. I never did think so. You know that."

"And you don't think Sebring did it, either?"

"No. I'm sure he didn't." Her voice had a queer catch to it.

I looked at her. "What makes you so sure?"

She said: "Duke, I've got something to tell you. Dr. Sebring didn't fall accidentally out your window. He was murdered."

I sat up. "Murdered?"

"Yes." Her face was white, as if she was remembering something damned unpleasant. "I—I looked his body over pretty thoroughly, there in the alley, before you ran up. And I found something."

"Found something?"

She nodded. Her fingers were trembling so she almost dropped her cigarette. "I found a stab-wound in his chest. He was knifed and then thrown out the window. Th-that's why I wouldn't let you go up to your apartment. I was afraid the murderer might still be up there and might—do something to you."

I said: "Good Jesus!"

Dixie sat on the edge of the bed alongside me. "Do you see what that means, Wop? It means the murderer is still somewhere close, and was afraid maybe Sebring would get his memory back and spill something dangerous."

I said: "Yeah, babe, but how did the killer know Sebring was at my joint?" Then, all of a sudden, I snapped my fingers and said: "Damn! I got it!"

"You've got what?"

"I've got the answer! I phoned District Attorney Terhune and told him Sebring was in my flat. And I told Terhune to get in touch with two women and have them come to my place to see Sebring and try and bring his memory back. Either of those two women might have croaked the little guy!"

"What two women, Duke?"

"Nelia Mason and Sebring's divorced wife!" I said.

Dixie stared at me. "Sebring's divorced wife? What has she got to do with it?"

I said: "Look, babe. Sebring's wife divorced him on account of the way he was running around with Myra Holly. Well, suppose Mrs. Sebring was still crazy jealous of him, even though they were separated. Suppose she walked into that surgery and caught him with Myra Holly and socked him, scrambling his brains. Then maybe Dr. Mason walked in and caught her in the act and she shot him. And, after that, Sebring got away before his ex-wife could finish up by croaking him, too."

Dixie said: "It's just as good a case against Mrs. Sebring as it is against Nelia Mason—except for one thing."

"One thing?"

"Yes. If Mrs. Sebring was the murderer, why would she cut up the dead woman in the surgery? There's no more sense to that than there is to the theory that Nelia Mason did it. Neither Mrs. Mason nor Mrs. Sebring would have any motive for destroying the dead girl's identity."

"Who the hell *would* have a motive for carving that dead dame?" I said. "That's the screwiest part of the whole damned case. And it's up to me to get going and find the answer. Here I am wasting time, when I ought to be out hunting up clues or something."

"You'll do your clue-hunting at night, when it's dark, Wop. Then the cops won't be so likely to spot you and drag you to the clink. And the murderer won't be so liable to grab you and maybe kill you."

"Hell, babe, why should the murderer try to bump me?"

"Use your brain. Suppose you were found dead, and it looked like suicide, and there was a forged note on your corpse, confessing that you were the killer? That would close the case—and the real murderer wouldn't have anything to worry about."

I said: "Jeeze, babe, you sound like a dime novel."

"Well, it might happen."

"The hell it might. I can take care of myself."

"Can you? You haven't done a very good job of it so far. Now look. I'm not going to let you go out of this room until after dark. You may as well make up your mind to it."

"That's a long way off. It isn't even noon yet."

"You can spend the time catching up on some sleep."

When she said that, I yawned, because I couldn't help it. Stretched out on the bed the way I was, I could feel my eyes getting heavy as hell. Dixie was saying something to me, but her voice kept getting farther and farther away and sort of buzzy in my ears. I guess I must have dozed off.

When I woke up, there was a red-orange light coming in around the sides of the pulled-down shade at the window, and I knew it was sunset. I moved around the bed, and my hand touched something soft and warm alongside me. I looked, and there was Dixie asleep, with her yellow hair all tossed and mussed on the pillow next to mine.

She must have slipped out of her dress to lie down with me and have gone to sleep, too, the same as I did. I stared at her. She wasn't wearing anything except silk step-ins with lace edges and a brassiere made out of some thin gauze stuff that let her white flesh show through. Her body was prettier that way than if she had been stark naked.

She had one arm thrown up over her head, and the curve of her armpit was mighty damned smooth and nice where it melted into the mound of her breast. Her eyes were closed, and the long lashes drooped and curled a little at the ends, and there was a sort of half-smile on her red lips. A strand of yellow hair was over on my pillow so that I could smell it, and it smelled sweet, like faint perfume.

She was breathing soft and gentle and easy, and her breasts moved just a little bit with every breath, and she reminded me of an angel, or something. And then I thought: what the hell, I'm getting mushy. I looked down at her flat stomach, all nice and smooth like satin, and her hips, that were curved just enough under her step-ins. And, below the step-ins, I could see her smooth white thighs, sort of spread apart a little, with one knee drawn up. Her legs were sleek through her silk stockings. I thought: God, she's pretty!

I couldn't help reaching out and touching her, and she opened her eyes sort of lazy-like and looked at me.

"Hello, Wop."

"Hello, Dixie."

"You didn't mind if I took a nap with you?"

"No, I didn't mind." I took her hand and held it. "Jesus, your fingers are nice and thin and smooth, babe."

"Oh, stow it, Duke. I don't want your flattery."

"I'm not flattering you. I mean it. You're sweet."

"You don't give a damn about me, and you know it. You think I double-crossed you and turned against you. You don't trust me."

"I don't know. Christ, Dixie, I wish I *could* trust you."

"What do you mean by that?"

"I mean I like you plenty, and I can't understand why you been acting so screwy toward me."

"I've been trying to help you and protect you, Duke."

"You took a funny way to do it, doping me and putting me on that boat."

"Maybe I had my reasons."

"Such as what, for instance?"

"I told you once. I've been afraid something might happen to you."

"Listen," I said. "You know something, don't you? You're holding something back."

"No. Honest I'm not." But she didn't sound very convincing.

I let go of her hand. "Sometimes I think, if I stick around you much longer, you're going to get me in plenty Dutch, babe."

She looked as if she was going to cry. "You poor dumb Dago fool, you think I'd put you on the spot? I—oh, I ought to throw you to the wolves and forget I ever knew you. Damn you, anyhow!" Her lower lip quivered.

I hate to see a dame bawl. Any dame. I said: "Aw, Dixie—forget what I said. I believe in you. On the level, I do." I kissed her on the mouth to prove it.

She put her arms around my neck. "Duke!"

I held her and patted her. "Turn off the tears, babe."

"I w-would if I c-could."

I kissed her again, and she sort of relaxed in my arms while I made love to her and, after a while, she closed her eyes like a tired kid. Pretty soon she was asleep again.

A long time afterward, she woke up and said: "I'm hungry."

"I'll get up and get dressed and go out and get us some sandwiches and a couple of bottles of beer. How does that sound?"

"No. You're staying right here until dark. I don't want you to go out while it's still daylight. I'll go for sandwiches."

"Well, okay." Then I thought of something. "By the way, babe, will you mail a letter for me?"

"What letter?"

"I got to write a note to Gertie Kohlar up in Fresno and send her that century."

Dixie looked at me sort of funny. "So you were thinking of her all the time you were holding me in your arms and making love to me! I might have known it, you Dago louse."

"Wait a minute. Don't get me wrong. I got to send that dough to keep Gertie from ratting on me and getting me in a worse jam than I'm already in."

"Oh, all right. Never mind the excuses. Write your letter."

So, while she was getting dressed, I wrote a note to Gertie on the hotel stationery, and slipped in the hundred bucks I'd got from the hock-shop. I gave the letter to Dixie. "Mail it right away, babe."

"All right, Wop, anything you say." Her voice sounded sort of tired and disgusted. She put on her hat and took the letter and went out of the room and closed the door after her.

I started pacing the floor. Now that Dixie was gone, I began to have doubts about her again. Besides, I had certainly pulled a boner by mentioning Gertie Kohlar so soon after making love to Dixie. Damn it, suppose Dixie got sore at me for that. Women are funny. Maybe she might go out and decide she hated me, and put in a call to the cops telling them where I was hiding out.

I decided maybe I'd better lam, just to be sure. But when I went to the door and tried to open it, I couldn't.

Dixie had locked me in.

Twenty-two

AT FIRST I thought she had done it to make sure I would be there when she sent the cops after me. But, on the other hand, maybe she locked the door just to keep me from wandering out before it got dark. I couldn't tell.

I thought of phoning down to the desk and telling the clerk I had been locked in by accident and would he please send up a bell-hop to let me out. But the clerk might think that was kind of screwy, and take a good look at me and recognize me from my pictures in the newspapers. Then he would know I was wanted by the law, and he would try to hold me until the bulls came. And then I would have to fight my way out, and maybe not make the grade, and then where would I be?

I went to the window and raised the shade and looked out. It was getting dark by that time, and it struck me that Dixie was staying out a hell of a long time just to buy sandwiches and beer and mail my letter to Gertie Kohlar.

I got a sudden idea where I might put in a call for help to get me out of that hotel room. I went to the phone and got the operator downstairs to put me through to Steve Kohlar's office. But there was no answer, because the office was probably closed for the night. So then I phoned the Kohlar house, and I recognized Joe's voice saying: "Hello?"

I said: "Is Steve there?"

I couldn't tell whether Joe tabbed me or not, but his tone got icy. "Yes. I'll call him."

In a minute, Steve was on the wire. I said: "Listen, boss. This is Pizzatello."

"For God's sake! Say—you can get in more damned jams than anybody I ever saw! Do you know the cops are looking for you again, and saying you knifed Sebring and pushed him out your bedroom window?"

"I figured they might think that, Steve. But I didn't do it. Honest. Hell, boss, why would I bump Sebring? I was counting on him to get me out from under this murder rap. If he could have got his memory back, he might have cleared me. Why would I croak him, when maybe he could have got me out of my jam?"

"Well, there's something to that. But you'll have a job making the D.A. believe you."

"Well, can you suggest anything, boss? You're a smart detective. Can't you give me some idea what to do next?"

"I don't know. There's one angle that's had me puzzled, Duke."

"What's that?"

"The bullet that went through Mason's skull and killed him. That slug was never found. And you claim it won't match your roscoe, like the two bullets they took from Mason's cork leg did. Now, if that death slug could be found, it might be a point in your favor. I've been working on that angle myself, to help you. I sneaked into Mason's surgery today and looked around, but I didn't get to make a very thorough search, because I heard somebody coming and had to duck out. So why don't you go down to the surgery tonight yourself, around midnight, and have a look around? If you go at midnight, you won't stand much chance of being nabbed."

"Jesus, that's an idea." Then I remembered my reason for calling Steve in the first place. "Say, boss. I'm in kind of a funny fix just now. I'm in a hotel room, locked in. I can't explain how it happened. Can you come up here and get me loose?"

"Sure. Where are you? I'll bring my skeleton keys."

I told him the hotel and the room number and hung up. Just then I heard a sound behind me. I turned, and there was Dixie in the doorway.

She had a paper bag under her arm. "Well, Wop, who you phoning?"

"Steve Kohlar."

"Why?"

I told her the truth. "I figured maybe you were mad at me and locked me in here so you could put the cops on my neck. I phoned Steve to come let me out."

"So you thought I was double-crossing you, eh, Duke?"

"Well, I didn't know."

She slammed the paper bag down on the bed, and the beer bottles rattled. "I locked you in so you wouldn't pull a dumb stunt and go wandering out before it was solid dark outside. But I might have known you'd think I was crossing you up. You're the type."

I began to feel sorry I hadn't trusted her. I said: "Well, anyway, babe, Steve gave me a good hunch to work on." And I told her what Kohlar had said to me.

When I got through, she said: "It sounds reasonable. But even if you find the bullet, how will you locate the gun it came from?"

"I don't know that. But the bullet would be a start. And I got to get going some place. I can't sit around here doing nothing."

"No, I suppose not."

"Well, then, I'll go to that surgery at midnight tonight."

"Why wait till midnight? It's dark now. Maybe you might find the bullet right away, and then we can get started on some other angle."

"We? What do you mean: 'we'?"

"I'm going with you, of course."

"No, you're not."

"Try and stop me, Wop."

"But why should you want to go with me?"

"Because I want to. Because—oh, nuts. I'm going with you, that's all."

"Well, okay then. Let's get going." I put on my hat and vest and coat, and we went out of the room and downstairs and out through a side door. We got in Dixie's little car, and she drove, and I sat close to her. Now that I was near her again, I wasn't suspicious of her any more. It was only when she was away from me that I got an idea she might not be leveling with me.

The night was plenty dark by that time, and Dixie drove down Madison Street where the medical court was. She parked around the corner from the front of the court, and we both got out and started walking toward the back entrance of the place.

When we got there, I took a look around, but didn't see anybody. All the bungalows were dark. I didn't catch any sign of cops or dicks hanging around, and that made me feel easier.

I took a gander toward the front of the court, and noticed a big Rolls limousine at the curb with nobody in it. I knew it wasn't a cop car, because cops don't go in for Rolls Royces, so it didn't worry me.

Dixie trailed along behind me as I made for the back door of the Mason-Sebring bungalow. Looking at that bungalow made me feel sort of shivery, because those two doctors had been alive and doing business only three days ago, and now they were both dead. A lot of screwy things can happen to people in three days, I thought to myself.

I tried the back door of the place, but it was locked. Dixie pulled a hairpin out from under her little hat. "I've picked locks before," she whispered. She got to work on the door, and after she'd fiddled with the hairpin for a while something clicked and she pushed the door open. "Come on, Duke. Don't make any noise."

We went into the little room where I had first gone the night of the murders. It was all dark and sort of spooky. I felt my way toward the door into the next surgery, where I had found those two corpses. Dixie had hold of my sleeve and was following me, and neither of us made any sound. Just as I reached the door into the second surgery, I saw a sudden glimmer of light in front of me.

My heart jumped in my chest, and my tongue got dry, and my throat seemed to tighten up. I grabbed for Dixie and shoved her back. I strained my eyes at the flicker of light ahead.

The door into the second surgery was halfway open, and I could see into the room where Mason and his broad had been croaked. I don't know whether I expected to see ghosts in there or what, but I felt queer as hell.

The light was flickering and dancing and wavering around, and it was sort of cold-looking and bluish-white. It gave me the creeps.

And then I saw it was a flashlight, and there was a guy in that surgery. He was flashing the light around, and he seemed to be looking for something.

Twenty-three

THE GUY'S FLASHLIGHT reflected back from the white walls and, when he turned around, I got a good gander at him. He was a big, tough-looking bird with a scar across his cheek, and he was wearing chauffeur's livery. Somehow, I kept thinking I had seen him before, but I couldn't remember where.

Dixie was trembling and holding onto me and digging her fingernails into my wrist so hard she almost drew blood. She was trying to drag me away from that partly open doorway.

But I stiffened myself and poked her with my elbow to be quiet. Meanwhile, the scar-faced guy flashed his light on a closet door, and went to it and pulled it open. The closet was on a line with the couch where I had discovered Mason's corpse.

I saw a shelf high up in the closet, and on it was a black leather Gladstone bag. The scar-faced chauffeur reached up and brought the Gladstone down and looked it over. He grinned a little, and then snapped off his light, and I heard him coming toward me in the darkness.

I grabbed Dixie, and pulled her away from the surgery door and made her crouch down alongside me. I put my arm around her waist, and my hand brushed up against her left breast, and I could feel her heart hammering under the firm, rounded flesh. She was shaking and trembling so I was afraid her teeth would chatter and give us away.

But the chauffeur didn't hear us, and went out through the front of the medical bungalow. I heard the front door closing after him.

I stood up and hauled Dixie to her feet. "Come on. We're tailing that guy."

"Duke—I'm afraid!"

"Nuts. I'm going to find out who he is, and why he wanted that traveling bag, and what it's all about."

Dixie and I slipped out the back door of the place and crept around front to see where the scar-faced man had gone. I looked toward the street and saw him getting into that parked Rolls Royce limousine at the curb.

When he got into the Rolls, all of a sudden I recognized him. I yanked Dixie back to the rear of the court, and we streaked across a vacant lot to the side street where Dixie's jalopy was parked. I said: "Get going and follow that Rolls!"

As she got under way, Dixie said: "Duke—who is that man?"

"I don't know. But I saw him once before, and it was right in this very neighborhood. It was the night Mason got croaked. I drove Mrs. Mason down here and, just as we turned into Madison Street, we almost bumped that same Rolls limousine. I got a squint at the chauffeur, and it was the guy we're following now."

"No!"

"Yeah. And I saw something else that night, too. There was a thin little grey-haired dame in the back of the Rolls. Nelia Mason saw her and ducked down and said something about knowing her."

By this time, Dixie had her car about half a block behind the Rolls, and we were following it toward the swell Oak Knoll district. Then, all of a sudden, the Rolls swung into the driveway of a big old-fashioned house and stopped under the portico. Dixie parked a little way beyond, and we both got out and strolled back along the sidewalk, very casual.

Just as we passed the house, I saw a dame on the wide porch. The verandah light over her head was on and I got a good look at her. My throat tightened up inside. It was the grey-haired dame who had been in the Rolls on Madison Street the night Mason and his broad got bumped.

Walking past the house, I heard the grey-haired dame saying something to the chauffeur. I just got part of it. "—won't need you any more tonight, William. You may have the evening off—"

He touched the peak of his cap and got back in the limousine. Dixie and I swung around and beat it to our parked jalopy. So when the scar-faced guy backed the Rolls out of the driveway and started off again, we were trailing right along behind him.

I said: "Babe, did you see that old biddy on the porch?"

"Yes. I saw her. She's—"

"She's the woman that was riding in that Rolls the night of the murders. She's the dame Nelia Mason recognized."

Dixie said: "I can tell you even more than that. I can tell you her name. I saw her picture in the newpaper today. She's Mrs. Willoughby Sebring. She's Dr. Sebring's divorced wife!"

I felt sudden sweat forming under my armpits. I said: "Jesus, babe! That means maybe we're on the right track at last! It's beginning to look as if she's the one we're after!"

Dixie said: "Maybe. But what about the chauffeur? What about that Gladstone bag he took from the surgery just now? I notice he didn't give the bag to Mrs. Sebring. He's still got it with him in the limousine. Where does he fit into the picture? And what's in the bag?"

"I don't know. But I sure as hell aim to find out. You keep trailing him," I told her.

We were out past Lincoln Avenue now, in a cheap residential neighborhood. Up in front of us, the Rolls turned down a side street and parked in front of a cottage that needed paint. The chauffeur got out and went up on the porch and opened the front door and went inside, carrying the traveling bag.

Dixie stopped her jalopy at the corner, and we sneaked back to the cottage. I saw a trickle of light leaking out a side window of the house through wide cracks in a blind drawn down over the open sash.

I pulled Dixie after me close to that open window. We looked in through the cracked blind.

The room was a bedroom, and I saw a woman lying on the bed. She was sort of young, and plenty good-looking, with soft brown hair, and red lips, and passionate-looking eyes. She was wearing a thin nightgown that was drawn up beyond her bare knees, showing her thighs. She was reading a confession magazine.

The bedroom door opened, and the chauffeur walked in and put the Gladstone bag on the floor and crossed over to the bed. He said: "How's my sweet baby tonight?"

"All right, but lonesome for you, sweetheart," the girl said. She put down her magazine and held out her arms, and the guy leaned over her and kissed her on the mouth.

"My little Myra-baby," he said.

Twenty-four

I FELT AS IF a mule had kicked me in the teeth. In the darkness, I turned to Dixie and whispered: "Jesus, babe. Did you hear that? *He called her Myra!* You know what that means? She must be Myra Holly!"

Dixie didn't say anything. She just pressed herself close to me and shivered all over.

My skull was full of pinwheels. If that brown-haired dame was the missing nurse who had worked for Mason and Sebring, then all my theories were shot to hell. Because, all along, I had figured the carved-up female in Mason's surgery was Myra Holly. But now everything was knocked into a cocked hat. Myra Holly was alive!

I looked in again through the cracked blind, and saw the chauffeur open his lips and clamp them over the girl's mouth and keep them there for a long time. His fingers were going all over her body, touching her every place he could think of. She had her arms around his neck, pulling him down toward her, and she acted like he was driving her crazy with his mouth and his hands.

I heard her saying: "Did Mrs. Sebring give you the night off, sweetheart?"

"Yes."

"You can be with me all night?"

"Sure. Sure, my little Myra-honey." He pulled down the shoulder-straps of her nightgown and bared her shoulders and kissed her on the throat and arms.

She started acting kittenish and teasing. She pushed him away and said: "Stop it. You don't really love me. All you want me for is—"

He said: "Don't love you? God, ain't I left my wife for you? I'm nuts about you."

She laughed, and kissed him and said: "Of course. I know you love me. I just wanted to see what you'd say."

"You knew what I'd say."

She wiggled her shoulders so the nightgown slipped plenty low. "You aren't sorry you left your wife for me, are you, sweetheart?"

"No. I ain't sorry. Are you?" He started touching her again with his fingers—here and there.

She shook her head. "I don't regret a single thing we've done, darling. Only—"

"Only what?"

"Well, one thing worries me. Why did we have to run away together the very night Dr. Mason was murdered?"

"That was just tough luck, baby. But it don't make no difference."

"No, except maybe the police will suspect me of killing Mason and that woman with him."

"Let the cops think what they damn please. You didn't kill 'em. That's all that counts."

"No. I'm not guilty, so nothing else matters, does it? But I'll have to stay out of sight a long while. If the police ever find me, they'll want to know why I disappeared the very night Mason was murdered. I'd have to explain how I'd run away with you, and you're a married man—"

"You won't never have to explain nothing. I keep telling you the cops think that carved-up woman was you. As far as they're concerned, you're dead. There ain't no more Myra Holly." He rubbed his scarred chin on her arm and shoulder and mauled her.

She played with his hair a minute, and then said: "Honey—"

"Yeah, baby."

"You—you went to the surgery tonight?"

"Sure."

"You got my Gladstone?"

"Yeah."

"You're sure nobody saw you? If they ever caught you in that place, they'd try to connect you with the murders."

"Nobody seen me; don't worry. I just went in the front door with the key you gave me, and took my flashlight and went to that closet you told me about. Your bag was on the top shelf like you said, so I dragged it down and brought it along. But I still don't see why you wanted it."

"I've got a good dress in it, and some other things. Personal things I used to keep there in the office. Bring me the bag and I'll show you."

He got off the bed, and crossed the room, and picked up the traveling bag and took it back to her.

She opened it, and dragged out a dress and some underwear and junk. Then, all of a sudden, I saw her eyes pop wide open and her fingers go to the bottom of the bag on the inside. She fumbled around and got pale as hell, and then she pulled something out in her hand and held it up. "Sweetheart—look!"

I saw what she had in her hand.

It was a bullet.

Twenty-five

IT WAS FLATTENED out of shape at one end and Myra Holly was holding it between her fingers, staring at it and breathing hard. The chauffeur's scar-marked face had turned sort of grey, and he looked plenty startled. But he was no more startled than I was.

I turned to Dixie and whispered: "Babe, for God's sake, do you see what I see?"

"Y-yes. Wh-what does it mean, Duke?"

"It means plenty! Unless I'm off my trolley, that's the slug that killed Mason!"

"Wh-what?"

"Yeah. Look. A slug went through Mason's skull and came out the other temple, and the cops couldn't find where it went. Neither could Steve Kohlar. Now we know why."

"You m-mean—"

"I mean everybody was looking for the bullet in the walls of the surgery. But it wasn't there. It was in that traveling bag. Here's what must have happened: the murderer shot Mason when Mason was on a line with the surgery closet. The closet door must have been open at the time. That Gladstone bag was on the top shelf of the closet, with one end sort of sticking off the shelf a little."

"Y-yes. Go on."

"Well, the bullet must have passed through Mason's noggin and spent itself by ploughing through a crease in the leather at the end of the bag, where it folds together. The slug stopped inside the bag, and that's where it's been ever since."

"But why wasn't it discovered before this?"

"Look in through the window, babe. Take a squint at that bag. When the bullet went in through the leather, the crease sort of folded around the hole, so nobody ever noticed it. Besides, the blow sort of knocked the bag back on the shelf, so it wasn't sticking out any more, see? When people started looking around the surgery for the bullet, that closet door was closed. The murderer probably closed it after the killing. Well, nobody thought to look inside the closet for the death slug, or, if they did, they didn't notice the bag standing far back on the shelf. And even if they had noticed the bag, they wouldn't have seen the hole in the leather, because it didn't show on account of the fold. Now listen, babe. You got a roscoe with you?"

"Yes. In my handbag here."

"Give me it."

Dixie opened her handbag and pulled out her little gat and handed it to me. I hefted it in my good left mitt, and gathered myself together, and took a flying flop at the open window of that cottage bedroom.

I hit the cracked blind, and it flew up with a hell of a racket. I landed on my knees inside the room. I was on my feet in a split second, and I pointed the roscoe at Myra Holly and the chauffeur. "Keep still, the both of you!"

Myra Holly started to scream. I jumped at her, and snatched the bullet out of her hand, and said: "Shut up, or I'll biff the brains out of you."

The chauffeur said: "You goddam son of a bitch!" and started at me, swinging his fists.

I could have plugged him, but I didn't want to, because there had been enough shooting in this case already. So I side-stepped, and kicked out with my foot and caught him in the groin. He let out a yeep and went down, holding himself.

Dixie scrambled in through the window. When she straddled the sill, her skirt went up around her thighs and I saw a lot of smooth white skin. She landed in the room and yelled: "Duke—be careful! Don't shoot anybody!"

"I won't unless I have to." I turned to Myra Holly on the bed. Her nightgown was down below her breasts, but she was so scared she didn't think to cover herself up. She just stared at me, with her jaw hanging open, and she was as pale as the sheet under her.

I grabbed her by the shoulder and said: "So that's why you wanted your traveling bag! You knew that bullet was in it, and you wanted to get it!"

"No!"

"Don't lie to me!" My brain was working at top speed and, all of a sudden, I got a new theory. I turned to the chauffeur and said: "You were in love with this Holly wren, but you knew Dr. Mason was getting gay with her, and you were jealous. So you got in Mason's surgery the night before last and croaked him. Mason had another dame in the surgery with him, and you bumped her, too, and carved her up, so she couldn't squeal on you. And you also biffed Dr. Sebring when he walked in on you, but he got away before you could get around to killing him."

From the floor, the scar-faced guy said: "That's a damned lie! I never killed nobody!" Then he groaned and grabbed himself again where I had kicked him, and he looked sick.

Then I whirled on Myra Holly and said: "Or maybe here's what happened: you were playing Mason, and you walked into the surgery and caught him with some other broad. So you croaked him and the broad out of jealousy, and biffed Dr. Sebring. And then you had to make a getaway, so you pretended to be in love with this chauffeur, and he fell for it, and brought you here where you could hide out."

Myra Holly said: "No! My God, no! I didn't do it! I swear I didn't do it!"

Then Dixie looked at me and said: "You're forgetting something, Duke. What about your theory that Mrs. Sebring was the murderer?"

That started me on a new track, and I spun around on my heel to face the chauffeur. "Yeah. That's right. Maybe it was Mrs. Sebring that did the killing—and you helped her."

The chauffeur groaned: "No!"

"Well, you drive for Mrs. Sebring, don't you?"

"Yes. I drive for her."

"And she was jealous of Sebring, even though she was divorced from him?"

"I don't know anything about that, Mister."

"The hell you don't. Anyhow, you were driving Mrs. Sebring along Madison Street near that surgical court the night of the murderers, because I saw you with my own eyes."

"Yes, sir. I was driving her along Madison Street that night. But we didn't stop at the bungalow court. Mrs. Sebring had been to a bridge party, and I was taking her home. That's the truth, so help me God."

I said: "Well, anyway, you and this Holly bimbo are mixed up in the case some way. I'm going to turn you both over to the district attorney. Maybe he can make you talk."

Myra Holly said: "You can't do that! It would come out in the newspapers that I ran away with a married man—"

"So what? Your rep isn't worth a dime a dozen, anyway. But maybe, if you come clean with the D.A., he'll cover up your elopement with this chauffeur guy."

"Come clean? I tell you I don't know anything! I haven't got the slightest idea who might have wanted to murder Dr. Mason. I— Wait a minute! I just thought of something."

"Yeah? You just thought of what?"

"I remember there was a woman who threatened to kill Dr. Mason."

"Oh, yeah?"

"Yes. She was a patient. She first came to Mason about six months ago. She thought she had appendicitis. She had pains in her right side."

"So what?"

"Mason examined her. Then he called me in and said he thought there was something very queer about her insides."

"Yeah? What was queer about 'em?"

"Well, Mason wasn't sure, but he thought her intestinal organs were misplaced. Transposed. He had me take her to an X-ray office there in the medical court, and we had pictures made of her abdominal region."

"Well, go on."

"The X-rays proved Dr. Mason was right. The woman wasn't suffering from apendicitis. She just had gas pains."

"How could the X-rays show that?"

"She couldn't have had appendicitis with pains on her right side, because her organs were really transposed. That happens sometimes. You've read of people having their heart on the right side instead of the left?"

"Yeah. Seems like I've read about cases like that."

"Well, this woman was that way. Only it wasn't her heart that was on the wrong side. It was her appendix."

"So what? Where does this get to?"

"I'm trying to explain as fast as I can. Like I just told you, Dr. Mason examined this woman. I saw her during the examination, and she had a lovely body. I guess Mason sort of fell for her, because, after he relieved her of the gas pains, she kept coming back to him for no reason at all. He started playing around with her."

"How do you know that?"

"Well, I walked in on them one evening in the surgery."

"You mean you caught them—"

"Yes. But I ducked out before they realized."

I said: "Well, what about this dame? When did she threaten to croak Mason?"

"Just a week or so ago. I was in the office, and this woman came in and said she wanted to see Dr. Mason right away. He took her into the surgery and closed the door, but their voices got pretty loud, and I caught snatches of what they were saying. She was telling him he had got her in trouble and she wanted money for an operation. He wanted to examine her to see if she was telling the truth, but she wouldn't let him. Then he refused to give her any money, and she got louder than ever and said, if he didn't come across, she would kill him."

"Then what happened?"

"He told her to get quiet, that he would try to dig up some cash. Then she went out. I don't know if she ever came back again. I never saw her after that."

"And who was this dame?"

Myra Holly frowned. "Let's see. I ought to remember that. I made out an index card of her case when she first came to the office. Her name was— Wait! Now I remember."

"Well, hurry up. What was her name?"

"It was Kohlar. Mrs. Gertie Kohlar."

Twenty-six

I STARED at Myra Holly. "Did you say Gertie Kohlar?"

"Yes."

"Spell it."

"K-O-H-L-A-R."

"You're sure?"

"I'm positive, now."

I felt dizzy all over. If the Holly wren was telling me the truth, it meant that Gertie had been playing me for a sucker all along. She had made me think I was the only man in her life, outside of her husband, and all the time she had been chasing around with Dr. Mason.

More than that, Gertie had claimed I got her in trouble, and at the same time she had told Mason he was the one. She had been working both ends against the middle and trying to blackmail both of us.

It began to look as if Gertie had never been in trouble at all. Otherwise, why would she refuse to let Dr. Mason examine her about it? She must have been scared he would find out she was lying.

And if she wasn't in trouble, why had she lammed to Fresno in such a hurry? The answer stood out like a sore thumb. *Gertie was the murderer!* She must have walked in on Mason that night in his surgery to get dough out of him, and caught him with another woman.

So she had croaked Mason and the broad and, when Dr. Sebring happened to come in accidentally and catch her in the act, she had biffed him unconscious with something heavy and stuffed him in a closet, figuring to come back to him and finish him off after she got through carving the dead dame. But when she went back after Sebring, he was gone.

That must have scared the pants off of her and made her lam to Fresno, and, because she needed dough in a hurry, she wrote me those two letters to scare me into sending some. And now maybe she was back in town, and had gone to my apartment to see me, and had found Sebring there, sick, and croaked him, tossing him out my bedroom window.

All this went through my mind in a second. Of course, if Myra Holly was lying, the whole theory fell flat. But, somehow, I had a hunch the Holly wren was shooting straight with me.

I looked at her and said: "Listen. If you're not leveling with me, God help you."

She said: "Why shouldn't I be telling you the truth? I've got my own neck to think about now."

"You're damned right. And while you're thinking about your neck, I'm thinking about mine. I'm taking you to see the district attorney, sister. Pronto."

"But—"

"No buts. Get off that bed and get dressed."

She looked at me, and looked at the roscoe in my fist, and then she pushed herself off the bed. She stood up and shrugged out of her nightgown and, when I saw her absolutely naked, I could understand why the scar-faced chauffeur went for her in such a big way. She had what it takes, and maybe some left over.

She grabbed a pair of panties and slid into them, and fastened a brassiere on her breasts, and put on stockings and shoes and a dress. While she was doing it, I spotted a telephone on the other side of the room, and I nudged Dixie, who was alongside me. I said: "Babe, go call up District Attorney Terhune at his house and tell him to meet us at police headquarters in fifteen minutes."

Dixie did what I told her and, by the time she hung up, Myra Holly was dressed and ready to go. I got the chauffeur up on his feet, and we all went out to Dixie's little car and got in.

Dixie didn't drive very fast, because we wanted to give Terhune time to get downtown ahead of us. When we finally parked in front of headquarters, he was just stepping out of his own sedan. He saw me and said: "What in the world—"

"Listen, Mr. Terhune. Let's go into your private office. This is damned important," I said.

He took us inside his office and looked us all over. "Just what is the meaning of all this? Who are these two people?" He pointed to Myra Holly and the chauffeur.

So then I spilled the whole story to him. I showed him the bullet that had come out of that Gladstone bag, and I made Myra Holly tell him everything she had told me. When she got through, I said: "Well, Mr. Terhune, I guess that cinches things. All you got to do is find Gertie Kohlar, and you'll have the Mason case sewed up tight."

He looked at me sort of funny and said: "Do you think so?" Then he got up and walked to the door of the office and said: "I want all of you to wait here until I get back. There's something I want to look into. He left us, and I heard the door being locked on the outside. So there I was, with Dixie and Myra Holly and the chauffeur, and none of us knew what was going to happen next.

I guess Terhune must have been gone an hour or more. It was close to midnight when he came back. The minute he walked into the room, I got a hunch things were haywire. His eyes bored into mine, and he said: "Well, Pizzatello, I'm afraid your theory won't wash."

"You mean you don't think Gertie Kohlar is guilty?"

"I am quite sure she isn't guilty," he answered, in that political-speech way he always used.

I said: "But how the hell can you be so sure?"

Terhune's voice got harsh as a buzz saw. "Gertie Kohlar isn't guilty, Pizzatello," he said, "because—she's dead!"

Twenty-seven

MY MOUTH TASTED COPPERY inside, all of a sudden. I stared at Terhune. *"Dead?"*

He nodded. "Yes. Thanks to the information which Miss Holly just gave me, I have succeeded in identifying the mutilated female corpse which was found in Dr. Mason's surgery night before last. Our original autopsy disclosed the abdominal organs to be transposed. And just now, while you have all been waiting here, I despatched two of my investigators to that X-ray office in the Medico-Surgical Court. They broke in and made a search, and they found the X-ray pictures which had been made of Gertie Kohlar several months ago. Those X-rays exactly match the organs of the mutilated woman whose body is now in the morgue. In other words—"

I whispered: "Jesus! In other words, Gertie's been dead all the time!"

"Quite."

I blinked my eyes. Terhune's office seemed to be pinwheeling around my noggin. I said: "But those letters she wrote me—"

Dixie grabbed my arm. "They must have been forged, Duke! Somebody imitated her handwriting!" Then she stiffened. "Oh, Lord—I've got the answer. *Joe Kohlar!*"

"Joe Kohlar?"

"Yes, Joe Kohlar! Look, Duke. Joe must have known about your affair with Gertie. And he must have known that she was chasing around with Dr. Mason, too."

"Yeah?"

"Yes. So Joe schemed to get even with all three of you. He must have followed Gertie to Mason's surgery that night. He killed Mason and Gertie, and hit Dr. Sebring over the head. He mutilated Gertie's corpse so she wouldn't be identified. Then he left everything so that you would be caught and arrested for the murders, while he went free!"

I said: "Wait a minute. How did he know I would walk in there?"

"Because he knew you were working for Nelia Mason to get divorce evidence for her."

"Christ!" I said. "Nelia Mason!" Then I whirled around to the district attorney. "Listen, Mr. Terhune. I'll catch your murderer red-handed, if you'll let me!"

"How?"

"You'll see. But you got to work with me. Remember, I'm in this thing up to my ears. If I fall down, I'm sunk. You got to give me a chance for my white alley!"

"I'm afraid I can't release you from custody, Pizzatello."

"I'm not asking you to release me. You'll stick right along with me. You and a couple of your men."

He thought a minute. "Well, all right. What is your plan?"

I said: "I haven't got time to explain it. We got to get moving right now."

Terhune put on his hat. "Very well." We started for the door. Dixie pushed herself up alongside me.

I said: "You stick here, babe."

"No. I'm going with you."

Terhune said: "I don't think that would be wise, Miss Parker."

"I don't care what you think. I'm going along!"

There wasn't any time to argue. I said: "Okay, babe." The three of us piled out of Terhune's office, leaving Myra Holly and the chauffeur inside. We locked the door on them.

Terhune got a couple of plainclothes dicks from the front office, and we all went out and got in a squad car. "Where to?"

I said: "Out Lincoln Avenue." And I gave the address of the cottage where I had found the Holly dame and her scar-faced boy friend.

It took us about eight minutes to get there. We left the squad car a block away, in an alley. We busted into the little cottage, and I rammed myself at the telephone in the bedroom. One of the plainclothes guys held a flashlight for me while I dialed the Kohlar house.

In a minute, I heard Joe Kohlar's voice saying: "Hello?"

I said: "Joe, this is Duke Pizzatello. Is Steve there?"

His voice froze up. "No. He went to a movie. He ought to be home pretty soon."

"Well, listen. As soon as he comes in, will you give him a message for me?"

"All right. What do you want me to tell him?"

"Tell him I need his help. I'm just about to crack the Mason case wide open."

"What?"

"Yeah. I've found out where that missing nurse, Myra Holly, is hiding out."

"The hell you say."

"And that's not all. The Holly bimbo *saw Mason and his broad being croaked!* That's why she took it on the lam. She's scared the killer will find out she knows so much. She's scared of getting bumped herself."

"For God's sake! You mean you've talked to Myra Holly, and she told you—"

"Nix. I haven't even seen her yet. I got my dope from another place. But there's no doubt about it. Myra Holly knows everything. And I got to have Steve's help."

"In what way?"

"Well, I want you to tell him to meet me at the corner of Lincoln and Fair Oaks as quick as he can. Then the two of us will go to the house where this Holly dame is

laying low. We'll nab her, and make her tell us everything."
And I gave him the address of the little cottage.

He said: "Okay. As soon as Steve gets home, I'll send
him to meet you at Lincoln and Fair Oaks. You wait there
for him. Maybe I'll come along with him."

"That will be swell of you, Joe." I hung up.

Terhune was right at my elbow. He said: "I think I'm
beginning to comprehend your plan. Your message just
now was not really for Steve Kohlar. It was to bait a trap
for Joe Kohlar. You believe Joe won't wait for his brother
to get home. Instead, you think Joe will come directly to
this address, so as to murder Myra Holly before she can
betray him. Isn't that right?"

I was too busy to answer him. I was arranging pillows
on the bed, and covering them with a sheet and a blanket
to make it look like somebody asleep there.

When I got through, I said: "Better station your men
where they can go into action fast, Mr. Terhune."

He nodded. He posted one of his plainclothes dicks in
the bedroom closet, and the other in the bathroom just off
the bedroom. Then he touched Dixie on the arm and said:
"Miss Parker, I think you had better go out to the au-
tomobile and wait there."

She hung onto me, pressing herself so close that I could
feel her breast flattening against me. "I'm staying right
here!" she whispered. She was trembling.

I slid an arm around her waist. "Take it easy, babe.
Everything's going to be okay."

"I—I'm scared, Wop."

I patted her. "There's nothing to be scared of." There
was a screen over in one corner, and I pulled her toward
it, and we both crouched down behind it. Terhune came
with us.

I don't know how much time passed, but it seemed like
a million years. And then, all of a sudden, I heard a sound.

Everything was solid dark in the room, and the noise
seemed to come from the window. I stiffened and held

tight to Dixie's little roscoe in my left hand, and then a round splinter of white light came from the window. It was the thin ray of a small pencil-flashlight.

The light jabbed across the room and fell on the bed and, in the reflection, I saw somebody slip over the sill and come inside. I saw a flash of white thigh under a skirt, and the glitter of a polished blue-steel gun-barrel in a clenched fist.

"A woman!" Dixie whispered. Just as she said it, there came a *"Chow-chow!"* from the blue-steel gun-barrel. Two orange-yellow streaks of fire reached out across the room to the bed, and the pillow-dummy jerked as the slugs hit it.

Then I was on my feet. I knocked the screen down and yelled: "Hoist 'em high!" At the same instant, Terhune started forward, and the plainclothes dick in the bathroom came bouncing out, with his flashlight brooming light across the darkness. The shamus in the closet snarled: "I got her—!" and closed in.

It was like prying the lid off of hell. I heard a roscoe stuttering: *"Chud-chud-chud-chud!"* four times, and the dick with the flashlight folded over, holding his guts. His light hit the floor and rolled. I brought up my own rod and squeezed its trigger, and felt it jumping against my hand while flame belched out of its muzzle. Then a slug stung into my right shoulder and spun me around, and I went down on my fanny.

Dixie was screaming, and Terhune was cursing, and the room was full of smoke and fire-tongues and roaring gun-reports. And then, all of a sudden, everything got quiet as a graveyard, and Terhune found the light-switch and snapped it on. The plainclothes dick from the bathroom was stretched out dead, and the other one was saying: "I got her, the bitch! I plugged her through the lungs!"

I managed to get on my pins and shake Dixie loose from me. I went over to a figure quivering on the floor and said: "This ain't no dame." I yanked away the hat and veil and wig and said: "Well, Steve Kohlar, I guess this ends the Mason murder case."

Dixie looked ready to faint.

ϟϟϟ

DIXIE SAID: "My God! *Steve* Kohlar! But I thought Joe—"

Steve looked up at me and coughed blood out of his punctured lungs and said: "You Dago bastard."

I said: "So you figured you could get away with this by wearing a dame's clothes, in case you happened to be spotted in the neighborhood, huh, Steve?" I picked up his blue-barreled roscoe where he had dropped it, and then I turned to the district attorney. "Mr. Terhune, you better get the two bullets out of that pillow-dummy on the bed. I'm betting my left ventricle they'll match up with the slug that killed Mason."

Terhune looked at me. "But I can't understand—"

I said: "The minute you told me it was Gertie Kohlar's corpse that was all carved up in Mason's surgery, I knew Steve was the guilty guy. He had to be."

"How did you figure it out?"

"I'll explain in a minute. But first, let's go back over the whole thing. The way I dope it out, Steve knew Gertie was playing around with Dr. Mason. She was his brother's wife, and he hated to see Joe fooled that way.

"Well, by luck, Nelia Mason came to the agency to hire a private dick to get divorce evidence against Mason. Steve assigned me to the case.

"Later that evening, Steve must have trailed Gertie to my apartment. He heard her tell me she was in trouble and wanted dough from me. So now Steve knew Gertie had been crooked with me, as well as with Mason.

"Steve also knew I had pumped a couple of slugs into Mason's leg that afternoon. He began to hatch a scheme to croak Gertie and Mason and pin the job on me. That way, he would be revenging Joe on all three of us—Gertie, Mason and me.

"Well, Steve probably tailed Gertie from my place to Mason's surgery, and he shot Mason and croaked Gertie and biffed Dr. Sebring, who must have walked in on the scene by accident.

"Then Steve took a scalpel and cut Gertie to pieces to rub out her identity. A little later, he fixed it for Nelia Mason to hire me again to get divorce evidence for her. Mrs. Mason didn't know her husband was already dead. Steve just used her as a tool to suck me into going to that bungalow court and being discovered with the two corpses. He knew my two slugs in Mason's cork leg would sure as hell convict me."

On the floor, Steve Kohlar coughed up some more blood and called me a Dago bastard again.

I went on: "Well, it all worked out the way Steve figured, and I got pinched for the killing. But a cog slipped when I got away from that cop in the surgery and lammed out to see Steve at his house.

"Steve knew that, if I found out the carved-up dame was Gertie, I would suspect either him or his brother Joe of the killing. That's why he had sliced Gertie to pieces in the first place. So, while I was in his house, he went into a back bedroom, saying he had to leave a message with Gertie for her to deliver to Joe."

"Yes. Go on."

"Hell, Mr. Terhune, it's plain as day. If Gertie was dead at the time, how could Steve go back into her room and leave a message with her?"

"He couldn't."

"Sure not. So, you see, he did that to fool me. He even imitated Gertie's voice answering him. A while ago, back in your office, when you told me Gertie was the carved-up corpse, I saw the whole thing. Why would Steve want to fool me into thinking Gertie was still alive, the night of the murders? What would be his reason, unless he was building an alibi for himself? *And why would he want an alibi unless he was the murderer?*"

Terhune said: "I follow you."

"Well, anyway," I went on, "that night Steve told me to go back to my joint and lay low for a while. He knew goddam well that, if I went home, the cops would trace me there and pinch me. Which they did.

"Then another cog slipped. Dixie, here, got me out of the jug. And Steve, in order to cover himself up, pretended like he was trying to help me. He even signed my bail-bond. And, in the meantime, he wrote me a phoney letter in Gertie's handwriting to make it look like she was still alive. He also wrote one to Joe. The chances are that Joe never realized the truth. He's probably home now, thinking Gertie's alive and visiting her sister in Chicago.

"But getting back to the morning after the murders: Steve knew Dr. Sebring had seen him in the act, and, when Sebring disappeared, it worried him. So, as long as I was out of jail for a while, he suggested for me to start hunting Sebring. He wanted me to find the little guy so he could croak him. Thanks to Dixie's damned fool stunt of shanghai-ing me, I ran onto Sebring and took him to my apartment. I phoned Joe Kohlar and told him I had Sebring at my place, and Joe must have told Steve about it. So Steve came up and croaked the little fellow. He figured that would help to tighten the rope around my neck, as well as shut Sebring's mouth forever.

"In the meantime, Steve wrote me another letter in Gertie's handwriting, and sent it to Fresno, and had it mailed to me from there. He probably figured the letter would scare me into trying to take a run-out powder; and for me to lam would be just like a confession I was guilty.

"But it didn't work that way, on account of because Dixie stepped in again to help me. She took me to a hotel and kept me free of the cops. Then I pulled another boner. I phoned Steve from the hotel, and he knew he had to do something else to put me in the grease. So he suggested for me to go to the Mason surgery at midnight and look for the bullet that croaked Mason. He probably figured to lay for me there and bump me and plant a phoney confession on me, or else he was going to trap me for the cops.

"Well, Dixie crossed him up by making me go to the surgery earlier, and it was a damned good thing. That's how we discovered that chauffuer, and followed him, and found Myra Holly, and got the whole case cleaned up."

Terhune said: "Then, when you phoned Joe Kohlar a while ago, you were actually giving a message for Steve, eh? You knew it was Steve for whom you were setting the trap?"

"Yeah."

Terhune looked at the dead plainclothes dick on the floor, and then he looked at Steve Kohlar. "Kohlar, since you've murdered a policeman before eyewitnesses, you'll hang. Well, you can't be executed more than once, no matter how many murders you've committed, so how about confessing the truth? Has Pizzatello reconstructed everything exactly as it happened?"

Steve said: "The Dago—bastard—got it—just about—right. But you—won't hang—me—damn you—*arg-g-gh!*" Something rattled in his throat, and blood gushed out of his mouth, and his eyes went wide open and sort of glazed. And that was the way he kicked the bucket.

About that time, I noticed my coat sleeve was all wet. Blood was dripping down the fingers of my right hand, and my wounded shoulder was beginning to pain like all hell. Also, I was getting wobbly at the knees from loss of blood.

I guess I staggered a little, because the next thing I knew Dixie was holding me steady, and there were tears streaking down her face, and she was sobbing: "Duke—you're hurt! Oh, Duke—!"

District Attorney Terhune said: "We'd better get you to a hospital, Pizzatello." Then he sort of smiled a little. "I imagine you'll be going on a honeymoon as soon as your shoulder is a little better, eh?"

Well, I hadn't thought about it, but, when he said it, I took a gander at Dixie and, all of a sudden, I knew I was nuts about her. So I said: "How about it, babe?"

She up and kissed me right there in front of Terhune and the plainclothes dick.

* * *

"Duke."

"Yeah, babe?"

"You know what day this is?"

"Sure. We been hitched three months today."

"You're sweet to remember. Listen. I've got a secret for you."

"What kind of a secret?"

"A nice one."

"Well, spill it."

"Can't you guess?"

"No. I'm a bum guesser."

"Well, then—how would you like being a papa?"

"Jesus, babe! On the level?"

"Y-yes—"

"Goddam! Ain't that something!"

"You mean it—it's all right?"

"Sure, babe. Give us a kiss."

She came to me, and I put my arms around her. And that's the way it was.